Heron
Mill

HERON MILL

THE BLACKWELL BROTHERS
BOOK ONE

K.L. TAYLOR-LANE

ISBN eBook - 978-1-7399897-6-7
ISBN paperback - 978-1-7399897-7-4
Written by - K. L. Taylor-Lane
Cover design by – Leah Maree at Designs by LM.

❀ Created with Vellum

Mother says I'm strange.

After hiding me away in a school for twelve years, her new husband wants me home. To be a family.

Out in the middle of nowhere, the Blackwell family's stone mansion stands tall. Heron Mill is hidden, tucked away deep in the forest, surrounded by nothing but trees. Something nefarious hides here. A sinister secret decaying in its basement.

And then there's *him*.

My new stepbrother is unusual.

The things he does, different. His behaviour, curious. The way his dark eyes watch me from the shadows when he thinks I don't notice, unnatural.

Wrong.

I can feel the darkness inside of him, cold and vicious. A sickness, something contagious, a poison seeping into my bones, disturbing something that long lay dormant. Something inside of me is starting to awaken and I'm really not sure it's something good.

For Daisy,
Because the first book I ever wrote was for you.

A NOTE FROM THE AUTHOR

Please be aware this book contains **many** dark themes and subjects that may be uncomfortable/unsuitable for some readers. This book contains **very** heavy themes throughout so please heed the warning and go into this with your eyes wide open.
For more detailed information, please see pinned posts on the author's socials.

The characters in this story all deal with trauma and problems differently, the resolutions and methods they use are not always traditional and therefore may not be for everyone.

This is an interconnected standalone. This book can be read unordered and as a completely separate entity to the other books in the series. However, for maximum enjoyment it is recommended you read in order.

CHAPTER 1
GRACE

The day is dreary. Heavy grey clouds loom overhead, light rain battering against my window. I stare out at the dense forest whipping by in a blur as the fancy car I'm seated in the back seat of flies down the road. I haven't been outside in a long time. I imagine the feel of the rain on my face, the smell of the fir trees filling my nostrils. Fat droplets of water splattering against my skin, running down my face. The cold wind rushing through my long, golden hair.

My hands clasped in my lap, I twist my bony fingers together. Scratching and picking at the skin around my nails, I halt the action immediately, knowing what Mother will say. She'll scold me for being *unkempt*. I place my palms on my thighs, smoothing down my dark green, plaid skirt, the gathers in the fabric perfectly pressed, exactly the way she'll expect. Or so Matron told me as she shoved me inside this vehicle and told me I was going home.

Home.

Such a strange word. I've never really had one before. Except for my special school. But that never really felt like home, wasn't much of a school either. I don't think. I don't have anything to compare it to. I've been at my school since I was six, I don't remember anything before that. Except for Mother's treatments.

A sharp feeling works its way into the centre of my chest at the thought, making me frown. I've been getting it a lot over the past few days. Since I found out I'd be leaving my special school to go *home*. I wondered if it was finally my time. If I was dying now that I'd turned eighteen. If it would hurt. If it would be slow. If I would drift off to sleep, never to wake again. Where I would go once I left this place. My body left behind, rotting and decaying, a decomposing buffet for maggots and flies and little beetles. Hopefully I'd be lain somewhere the insects could find me. Or the foxes. I rub my thumb over the centre of my chest, trying to force the tightness away, feeling it spread through me like a heavy, dark shadow. Something cold and foreign.

I continue watching the forest rush by, the rain coming down harder as the day morphs into night. The rain never letting up once, I let my eyes slip closed, tired of travelling to the unknown. My school was in woodland too, the old brick building was set miles from anywhere else. Harder to run that way. On our journey we've passed through places with much larger buildings than my school. Some were so tall they reached all the way into the thick grey clouds, their fluffiness overshadowed with darkness. A curtain pulled over the sun. When we passed through where the buildings were, it was noisy and busy and there were so many people that I had to look away. It gave me that feeling in my chest again.

Maybe I really am dying.

"We've arrived, Miss."

My eyes pop open as the car rolls to a stop, the driver unclipping his seatbelt and stepping out of the car. The sky outside now pitch, I squint through my rain covered window, trying to look out, but all I can see is my own darkened reflection. My breath fogging the window, I press my fingers to the cool glass. Tracing a small *G* in the centre with my fingertip just as my door is pulled open.

I release my restraint, twisting my bottom around on the seat, placing my small fingers in the driver's awaiting palm. He assists me out of the car, shielding me from the rain with a large umbrella. I brush down my skirt, straightening the white collar beneath my black, woollen jumper, as he leads me towards a staircase.

I stop dead in my tracks, the driver's footsteps crunching forward over gravel without me. Craning my neck back, I stare up at the huge stone building. Thick green ivy covers one half of it, the windows almost invisible beneath. All of the oversized windows lit up from the inside, warm honey shining through, illuminating the area surrounding it. A wide, open-mouthed, stone staircase leads up to an enormous front door. A deep cherry red wood with a brass knocker in the shape of some sort of creature. I have to strain my neck back so far to even glimpse the top floor of the house. I don't know how tall this building is.

If there's one thing I *do* know, it's that this is not my old house. I may not remember much about where I lived before, but I would remember if it were here. I suddenly wonder if I'm not going back to Mother at all. Perhaps Matron was lying about Mother wanting me to come *home*. Perhaps this is a new school instead. A boy at my school, Timothy, he would read to me sometimes. He told me a story about a girl living in a castle once, and the scary beast that laid within. Timothy would never finish the story. It was very unsatisfying when he got to the parts he thought were scary and wouldn't continue. Those were always the parts I wanted to know about.

I close my eyes, letting the rain cascade over me. My jumper soaked through, my bare legs running with water, I just stand here. Everything around me silent but the sound of the now hammering rainfall. Embracing the feel of the howling wind slapping against my wet face, my lashes heavy with water. A sharp tug on my wrist drags me back to the present. My eyes snap open, my chin dropping, I tilt my head in observation at the woman standing before me.

The driver stands to her left, holding the same large umbrella over her head. Her hard stare bores into me. Those hazel coloured eyes that match one of my own, pale blonde hair coiffed in delicate curls around her shoulders. A royal blue cardigan draped over her thin shoulders, a white blouse beneath, tucked into a dark pencil skirt. I take it all in quickly before dropping my gaze.

"Grace, you're absolutely sopping wet! Get in the house," Mother snaps, her delicate fingers curled around my thin wrist, long nails snagging my pale skin.

I swallow the lump in my throat as she turns, dragging me behind her, her grip tightening so hard I wince. My feet scuffing against the wet gravel, small stones from her heels flicking up at my bare shins like little missiles. She marches me up the stone steps, the driver keeping pace to preserve her at all costs. The needling in my chest returns with a vengeance. My toes scuff against the steps as she drags me up behind her like she used to do when I was a little girl. When we reach the top, she gives me a hard shove inside the open door, releasing her hold on me. My hands automatically clasp together before me, my unmatched gaze she hates so much instantly dropping to the floor. I try to breathe slowly as I study my wet feet, my old, battered Converses soaked right through to my frilly, white ankle socks. I bite my lip, tugging it inside my mouth, clamping it between my teeth.

I blink hard, my body trembling as I stand stationary, awaiting instruction. Or dismissal. I'm not very good at understanding people's reactions to things. Something as simple as my being wet from the rain has flared something dangerous inside of Mother. I should have stayed under the umbrella, kept pace with the driver. Mother's heels clack against the dark wooden floor, echoing down the hall as she moves away from me.

My shoulders tense the longer I wait, my neck pinching from being angled down for so long. The cold from my wet hair and clothes seeping into my bones, making my teeth chatter. I clench my jaw, locking it shut to quiet the sound. My body trembles as her heels re-approach, another set of footsteps with her. The echoing growing louder as she approaches with the newcomer. I know my place, so I keep my eyes averted, seeing nothing but the entrance hall floor and my muddied, fraying shoelaces.

"Ah, here she is!" a smooth, deep voice says with something akin to joy in his tone, a loud clap of hands accompanying the words.

It's such an unusual reaction to my presence that I unintentionally flinch, the needles pricking inside my chest again. I want to run my knuckles over the place the feeling twists, but I refrain.

"Grace," Mother coos, so softly that you'd wonder who this new woman is.

Like a different spirit crawled its way inside of her shell, her body appearing back before me with a completely new personality.

Acting.

A lie.

Matron says we mustn't tell lies. Lies always get found out in the end, even the little white ones, *fibs* are also punishable.

The way she says my name, like it has meaning. Like I'm a *person*. It makes me feel... *strange*.

Still staring at the floor, I shift my weight from one foot to the other. My sodden shoes squelching with my movements, the rubber sole squeaking against the polished wood floor. I curl my toes, the wet cotton of my socks clumping between them uncomfortably. My fingers flexing, short nails cutting into my palms as I squeeze them into fists. I don't know whether I should look up or not. Indecision wars inside me, Mother telling me not to look her in the eye, because I'm strange and my eyes unnerve her. Matron telling me to focus on someone's face when they speak to me. The lashings that followed when I didn't.

"Grace," the male voice echoes Mother's, breaking my dangerous train of thought.

Shined loafers take a bold step towards me, his toes a foot from mine, stopping just at the edge of the little puddle of water that's formed around me.

"Grace, where are your manners?" Mother shrieks. "Look at Mr Blackwell when he's speaking to you!" she tuts, a small scoff of laughter leaving her lips.

I've never heard anything quite so odd coming out of her before. That alone is enough to get my head snapping up. I squeeze my fingers, my gaze falling upon a handsome man.

A very *tall*, handsome man. Broad shoulders, a full head of wavy black hair, dark eyes and olive skin. Stubble on his jaw and chin, perfect lines, so it's not that he hasn't shaved, he wants to keep it that way. A pale blue dress shirt pulled taut across his chest, sleeves folded neatly to his elbows and black, pressed slacks on his legs.

"Welcome to Heron Mill, Grace," he smiles warmly.

I blink up at him, he's not in my space, but he's definitely a little closer than most people tend to stand in my presence.

"Grace!" Mother scolds this time, her true tongue spitting the words.

"Thank you, Mr Blackwell," I rush to reply quietly, swallowing hard.

Mr Blackwell turns ever so slightly; giving Mother a stern look that I can't quite interpret, but I can feel the power rolling off of this man in waves. I want to shrink back, but I don't, knowing that whatever interaction has just taken place is, for once, not aimed at me.

"Please, Grace, no need for formalities, you can call me Stryder. I am your stepfather, after all," he chuckles, and I blink.

"My-"

"Oh, Stryder! I haven't had a chance to tell her yet!" Mother laughs, cutting me off, the sound shrill, making my ears ache.

She steps up beside Stryder, swatting at his wide chest, pressing her body up against his thick arm. Her pale pink nails press against the fabric of his shirt as she wraps a hand around his bicep.

"What do you mean, you haven't told her yet? We've been married for six months, you said she couldn't attend the wedding because she was unwell," he questions and accuses, his tone deep and sharp.

My eyes flicker between the two of them, my feet subconsciously shuffling me back half a step when I catch the look of pure hatred on Mother's face. It's gone as quickly as it appears, but I saw it. I'd know that look anywhere. That's something I couldn't forget if I tried.

Mother clears her throat, Stryder staring her down with a deep frown as I take another step back. Wondering whether I should just take my chances out in the rain tonight. Leave them to discuss whatever it is that, well, *hasn't* been. It's been so long since I've been free to explore the outside that I'm sure I'll enjoy it. I smooth my hands over my skirt, my skinny fingers sweeping over the thick fabric as I take another small step away. Mother and my *stepfather* speaking quietly to one another. Just like if I weren't here. If I just go back outside, I can disappear off into the forest for hours. Although, it is cold, and my jumper is already wet.

"Let me get Rosie to show you to your room, Grace. Get you some dry clothes and something to warm you up. How does that sound?" Stryder asks loudly, startling me from my thoughts as his deep voice echoes around the large entryway.

I nod once in response. My gaze safely diverting back to my feet. If I just don't look, she'll forget I'm here. This is a big house, I'm sure I could busy myself enough to keep out of her way. Dependant on where my room is of course…

Stryder and Mother leave me under the supervision of Rosie the housekeeper, Mother having given her strict instructions about my pills. Rosie smiles at me. An older lady, plump around the middle with a fast pace and even quicker tongue. Her greying hair pulled back in a tight braid, wound around her head like a silver crown. I eye it as she steers me through the huge stone house, wondering how she gets it to stay that way. I almost have to run to keep pace with her as she explains the history of Heron Mill to me. Rattling off facts about the nineteenth century watermill. Not that I can pay full attention to her as she weaves us through various corridors and hallways, I'm far too interested in taking in my surroundings.

Deep regal red carpets with a demask pattern line the centre of the wooden floors. A mix of textured wallpapers and exposed stone walls are revealed as we make our way up a second set of stairs. Rosie leads me down a darker hallway, closed doors on either side, small stone sconces on the walls. We finally come to a stop before a door at the very end. Rosie removes a large iron key from her front apron pocket, pushing it into the lock and twisting twice before pushing open the door.

"Here we are," she exclaims, making her way into the room first.

Flicking on a couple of lamps as she moves around the oversized room.

"Well, come on in, deary! We need to get you out of those wet clothes and into a warm bath. How do you take your tea? Milk? Sugar? Earl Grey okay for you?" she fires off the rapid questions, my mouth working to respond, no actual sound coming out.

She bustles back through the room, stopping before me when I stay rooted at the threshold.

"Pretty, isn't it?" she hums cheerfully.

Leaving me where I stand, instead, crossing back over to what appears to be a bathroom. Steam billowing out of the open door as I hear the rush of water start to fill a bath.

I nod silently, even though she can't see me, still taking in the expansive space.

A huge bed sits along one cream wall, dressed in pale blue sheets, little bumblebees embroidered on the linen. The wooden headboard carved out with a woodland scene. Matching dresser and wardrobe along the opposite wall, set either side of the bathroom door. An arched window takes up most of the rear wall, an overstuffed armchair placed before it, looking out over the view currently shrouded in darkness. A small table complete with reading lamp beside it.

Rosie hurries back out of the bathroom, a pile of fluffy towels in her hands. She places them down on the end of the bed, turning sharply to face me, her hands placed on her wide hips.

"What are you doing still standing there? Get in that bathroom and strip those wet clothes off before you catch a chill!" she barks the order and I hurry to comply, still not knowing the rules of my being here.

I don't know what I'm allowed to do, where I can go, how long I'm going to be visiting for. Hopefully I will find out in the morning. I assume it must be quite late now, considering I left school before sunrise and it's already pitch dark outside. I'm sure someone will explain how things are to me in the morning.

The bathroom is all white, the floor tiles running up and over the walls. A large glass shower along one wall, a toilet and twin sinks the other, a claw foot tub in the centre. Unlacing and toeing off my Converses, I peel my wet clothes from my cold skin, letting them go splat against the tiled floor, I drop them into a heap.

Resting one trembling hand on the edge of the large bath, I dip my toes of one foot into the lavender scented water. Hissing at the heat, I wince as it singes my toes, but I know not to be difficult, so I force myself to place both feet in. My attention flitting back to the cracked door every few seconds, I really don't want to be forced into this water if I can help it. I inhale sharply through my nose, my pale skin instantly turning bright pink as I lower myself into the scalding water, my lip tucked between my teeth to keep my squeak in.

When I'm finally submerged into the lava temperature water, I hear Rosie making her way inside the bathroom. I twist my head over my shoulder, watching as she hurries in with a silver tray, a teapot perched atop it. A folded table beneath the other arm. She sets it all up beside me, mumbling to herself about how I look as though I need two sugar cubes instead of one and then proceeding to drop in a third. She stirs the murky coloured tea, placing the silver teaspoon onto the saucer. Offering it up to me, I take the small tea cup from her, blowing steam across the top of it.

I flick my gaze, watching her from the corner of my

eye as she lays towels over a heated rail. She moves around like she doesn't know how to sit still. Nobody's ever done things for me before. I stare back at the icky coloured drink in my cup, wondering how I can get rid of it without having to swallow it. I hate tea. With Rosie's back turned, I tip my cup, dumping its contents out into the bath water with me, quickly placing it on the little table as she turns back.

Once Rosie deems me clean and soaped enough to drain the water, I get out of the bath. She tried to make me drink two more cups of tea. I actually had to sip the third cup and I still can't get the horrible taste out of my mouth.

I sit on the corner of the bed, wrapped up in three huge fluffy towels, drowning me inside them. Watching as Rosie pulls open drawers like it's a competitive sport, filling her arms with various items of clothing. She turns back to me, laying out some sleepwear for me to choose from. I frown hard, blinking back up at her. Overwhelmed with being asked to choose. I'm not allowed to be fussy. What if I choose the wrong thing? What if I'm not really supposed to choose at all?

The needles in my chest poke at me again, my tongue trying to wet my dry lips.

"You can wear whichever you want to, Grace. The choice is yours," Rosie says suddenly, breaking me free from my thoughts. "Or I could choose for you tonight?" she asks, her green eyes monitoring me closely.

I swallow, nod, blink.

She smiles then, softly, gathering up everything from

the bed except for a set of silky white pyjamas. A pair of long pants, a long sleeve, button up, collared shirt and white cotton knickers. Disappearing back into the bathroom, humming under her breath, I stand, dropping my wet towels. I stare out into the darkness as I pull on the soft clothes, their silky texture so different than what I'm used to. I usually have thick, scratchy materials and wool. Everything is rough and itchy. Such a stark difference to these. I approach the window as I start to button my shirt, pinching my eyes to try and see farther out. But it's too dark and the light in the room only allows me a view of my own reflection, my oddly coloured eyes staring back at me.

I drop my gaze, smoothing my hands down my top, reaching up to tuck my long hair behind my ears. I sweep the thick golden tresses over my shoulders, letting their damp ends slap the top of my bottom. After Rosie sits me down at the dressing table and brushes through my hair, drying it, and braiding it in two, she hands me a palm full of pills and a bottle of water. Watching as I swallow them down, she smiles, tucking me into bed before switching off the light. The door clicking shut gently behind her as she leaves.

Then there's just nothing.

There's no shouting or screaming. No doors or shackles banging and clanking. No heavy breathing from a hidden dark corner. No tears or tantrums or manic laughter.

There's just *me*, and the rain against the window.

The fat droplets hammer against the glass, trees

rustling as the wind whistles through them. I stare up at the ceiling, from the too big bed that threatens to swallow me whole as I melt into the feathered blankets and pillows.

That's when I realise, there was no key turned in the lock. I didn't hear it.

My heart beats fast, thumping inside my chest, my ribcage rattling with the force of it.

I turn my head to the left, staring through the heavy cloak of darkness like I can make myself see the door. *Know*, if it is indeed, unlocked.

Indecision wars within me. The prickles in my chest picking up as I push my covers back. Swinging my legs over the side of the bed, pressing my feet into the thick rug, I curl my toes. My fingers gripping the edge of the mattress, I finally push up, cautiously taking a step towards the door that I can't see, but know is there. When the wooden floor beneath my feet makes no sound under my weight, I continue forward. Blindly crossing the large room. When I reach it, my hands outstretched before me, ensuring I don't walk into it, I grasp for the handle. My fingers grip the door knob, my chest so full of needles now it feels like a hedgehog crawled up inside me to live beneath my ribcage, but it changed its mind and now it's trying to break free.

Taking in a deep breath, I push the handle down and pull it gently toward me. The door opens. I blink into the darkness, the door open no more than a crack before I decide to click it closed and hurry back to bed. My heart thumping like a wild horse galloping in my chest. I tear the covers up to my chin, my fingers knotted in the soft sheets.

Why isn't my door locked?

Mother would never let me stay with her without my door being locked. Even at school we were locked in, sometimes tied down to our beds with leather cuffs on our ankles and wrists. Large straps banded over our thighs, tummy and chest. Thinking of all the possible reasons why the door would be left unlocked, I finally settle on it being an accident and close my eyes.

CHAPTER 2
HUNTER

The clouds are low, thick and heavy with rain just waiting to burst free. Lady gallops faster, trampling over exposed roots and mushrooms, flattening wildflowers beneath her hooves. Clinging onto her bridle, my knuckles locked, fists clenched. Her triceps bunch and flex beneath my clenched thighs. The feel of her strong form working beneath me never fails to amaze me. Shire horses are notoriously gentle creatures, Lady is no exception. Unless you try to saddle her. She doesn't like to be ridden with equipment.

The first drops of rain hit my face, a deep rumble of thunder rolling off in the distance. I lean forward, Lady picking up her pace, shooting us through the dense trees. The sky darkens further, making it a struggle to see, lightning flashing up ahead lights our path for a split second and then we're breaking through the trees. Artificial lighting from the stables is our homing beacon, calling to us like a silent siren, we make it into the dry.

Dismounting and making sure everything's closed up, I make my way towards the back of the house. My footsteps heavy, muddied boots weighing me down, I stop and stare up at the ostentatious house that's been built over the top of the old mill. The back of the house is full of large windows, overlooking the brook and stream, that once upon a time, were used to turn the turbine. When the mill was still in operation it was used to make flour. Now that crumbling building is the basement of Dad's new house, with a few special adaptions, of course.

Light flares to life in the furthest back bedroom on the top floor. I tilt my head watching, waiting for whoever is inside to show themselves. No one uses that section of the house. Like most of the second floor. Since my brothers, both younger and older, moved out, it's been left empty. Abandoned. Nothing but ghosts traipse through there these days. A shadow dances to life on the far wall, *Rosie*. I watch as she bustles about, doing who knows what in the empty room. Most likely Dad's *wife* has got her doing something ridiculous. The woman's a bitch, treating everyone that works here like her own personal slaves. I'd take her down into my basement in a heartbeat if Dad didn't like her so much.

Soaked right through, my long-sleeved t-shirt clinging to my body, my jeans heavy and tight. I blow out a breath, my body heat reflected back to me in a puff of condensation that appears in the cold air. It's cool for September, it's usually warm this time of year. But as is typical of English weather, it isn't. Not today anyway. Restarting my journey back into the house I spare one last glance up at Rosie and stop dead.

A girl stares out at me. Skin so pale it reflects like the face of the moon. Hair like spun gold, so long and thick it swallows the rest of her up. I step closer, my neck arching back, I get as close as I can without losing my view and then she turns away. I blink and she's gone. My heart thuds hard in my chest, rain running into my eyes, I blink it away, my skin tingling with *something*. I swallow hard, taking a slow, deep breath, I head into the house.

My boots thump as I make my way through the quiet house. Everyone having already retired to their suites for the night. This is my favourite part of the day. When the staff are all finished and have gone to bed. Dad and his wife are locked away in their wing. I get to float down the halls like a ghost. A spectre. A phantom. Nothing more than a shadow among shadows in the old house.

I take the wooden stairs down into the basement. More darkness greets me as I reach the bottom, pushing open the wide door, creaking on its hinges. I let it shut behind me, then flick on the desk lamp. Original grey stone floor and walls, the old millstone off to the left, bed to the right. Door at the far end leading to a small space, fitted with vents and drainage, a furnace. Metal mortuary table taking pride of place in the centre of it all.

I peel my t-shirt up and over my head, balling it up, I toss it onto the back of my leather armchair sat beside the fireplace. My skin pebbling with goosebumps, I unbutton my jeans, pushing them and my boxers down my legs, kicking them off along with my muddy boots. I grab a towel from the shelves, running it over my shaggy black hair. Shaking it out, little droplets of water flying free. I rub the towel over my chest, rolling it down each leg, before I drop into my chair. I lay my head back, my eyes closed, allowing the wet towel to fall free from my fist, dropping to the floor.

Who was that girl?

My brothers don't live here anymore, so it's not someone they brought home. When they lived here it was always Archer who had an abundance of women around him. Our oldest brother Thorne was always scolding him to be more discreet, telling him not to fuck women wherever the hell he felt like it. He never did seem to listen, he just chose darker corners of the house to claim his conquests, before ushering them away again. Nothing seems to hold his attention for too long. Quite like my own.

I've never felt any attraction to women. Or men. I've never really felt anything towards *anyone* before.

Until now.

But this is not attraction. I wasn't nearly close enough to get *that* good of a look at her. Although, what I did see I didn't exactly *dislike*.

I scrub a hand over my face, pushing my fingers through my black hair. My eyes squeezing shut, I pinch the bridge of my nose, exhaling a deep breath.

It's intrigue.

That's all it is. A curiosity. One that can be snuffed

out, as easily as trampling over dandelions. I don't need to obsess over how her pale skin shone like the brightest star in the night's sky, or how her long golden hair reminded me of sunflower fields. How I imagine running my fingers through the thick strands, knotting it around my fist. Nuzzling my face into the side of her pale throat, her skin caught between my teeth.

My cock hardens to steel, surprising me as it bobs up against my lower belly. I will it to go down without needing attention. Sinking my teeth into my lower lip, I drop my head back against the worn leather of the chair. My fingers digging into the square arms, knuckles cracking with the pressure. I've never had this sort of situation before. I don't ever need to do *that*. I've made it to twenty-five without ever needing to touch myself. I'm not about to start now over a tiny girl with too much hair.

So thin and fragile, dwarfed by all that hair and then some. An outfit of clean white. It would look so pretty if I dirtied it up, smeared it with crimson as I tore through the material with my hunting knife. The blade nicking at her creamy skin.

I groan into the darkness, throwing myself out of my chair. Uncertainty rides me hard, a need I've never had before overtaking every rational thought I've ever had. My fists curling and flexing at my sides, I huff out a loud breath. Pacing my room, my damp feet cold against the harsh stone floor. My dick gets harder and harder the longer I walk back and forth. Fisting my hair, I stop in the centre of the room, staring down at my raging erection. My dick so hard it could punch through concrete.

This is all *her* fault.

Grabbing a pair of jogging bottoms from my dresser, I throw them on and head out of my room. The darkness of the silent house engulfs me, the shadows welcoming me as one of their own. A familiar, a predator, the thing that goes bump in the night. Without needing my eyes to adjust I make my way through the sleeping house, striding towards the back stairs, winding my way up the curved staircase without a single thought of what I'm doing. Something inside me compels me forward, moving my feet without any conscious effort at all. Before I know it, I'm stood before the door. The closed door which leads to the furthest bedroom in the back of the house.

I stand stock still, staring at the wood, my eyes momentarily flicking down to the handle. I raise my fist, slowly uncurling my fingers, placing my palm against the door. Silence surrounds me, a low buzzing that could just be inside my head. I can hear my pulse hammering away in the side of my neck, blood pounding through my veins. Feel my heart thudding erratically in my chest, my lungs working overtime. I've never felt more alive. Everything in me somehow already knowing that whatever is about to happen is going to kick-start a chain of reactions I can't even begin to comprehend. And nothing good is going to come from it. Swallowing, I place my ear to the door, holding my breath, straining to listen.

Silence.

No shuffling, no breathing. I hear absolutely nothing at all.

I frown hard, my dark eyebrows dipping low, my fingers find the brass handle, easing it down. I feel the catch release, my muscles tense, freezing my movements for a moment, knowing that all I have to do now is push my way inside. This is too easy. There's zero resistance as I slowly nudge the door open, no more than a couple inches at a time, revealing nothing but darkness on the other side. I take it slow, my breathing picking up a little as the door opens just wide enough for me to slip through.

And then I'm inside. I blink hard, narrowing my eyes on Thorne's old bed. The wooden headboard I know to be carved in a woodland scene, complete with lake, heron and fawn. A small bump lies in the centre of the mattress. Smothered by light sheets, cloaked in darkness, rain lashing against the huge observatory style window. A single flash of lightning forces the room into the brightest light, a split-second flash reveals the girl.

Knowing I should leave, I make my way closer, an invisible tether drawing me in. My feet sweeping silently over the wood and rugs alike, until I'm towering over her sleeping form.

Like Death came by to view an angel.

A clap of thunder directly overhead, an immediate bolt of lightning. The room brightens like the sun once more, but she doesn't even stir. The quilt cover is only pulled up halfway, folded down just below her sternum.

Her thin arms encased in white silk lie flat over the folded covers like she got hot and threw them back in her sleep. Her dainty hands delicately poking out of the too-long sleeves. A sliver of her pale chest exposed in the V neckline of the button-up shirt.

I lean forward, unable to stop myself as my eyes finally adjust to the dark. I trace a finger over the exposed portion of her collarbone. Her hair in twin braids, corded like rope on either side of her head. Her breathing deep and even in her chest, her ribs expanding and contracting slow and steady. My gaze flicks up to her closed eyes, heavy black lashes shadowing her cheekbones, fanned out over her thin face. No creases on her brow, no tension in her face, no lines or blemishes on her alabaster skin. So silken and soft, utterly *perfect*. I haven't had the pleasure of peeling back skin as quintessential as this, well, probably ever. So flawless, it makes my breath catch in my throat. My knuckles slide along her jaw, her body lain slack, her sleep so deep I don't think a bomb going off would wake her.

My other hand effortlessly slips beneath the waistband of my joggers, taking hold of my throbbing dick, squeezing until a bead of pre-cum rolls down my tip and onto my thumb. I draw in a deep breath, gritting my teeth, as I start to roll my hand down my thick shaft, teasing the foreskin up and over my crown. My movements increasing as the fingers of my other hand continue to dance across the soft skin of her face. Her gentle breaths puffing from between her slightly parted lips. So thick and plump, the perfect pout, a deep cupids bow. More lightning, a boom of thunder as the storm circles directly overhead. My breathing picks up, the pad of my thumb applying the smallest amount of pressure to her thick bottom lip.

My chest aches, something in my lower belly twisting and tightening. I stare down at her perfect face, small nose slightly upturned, a single freckle beneath her left eye. More pre-cum oozes from the tip of my steel cock, my fingers flexing, my grip tightening. Using a corkscrew motion, I tug at my cock aggressively, my movements erratic, hips thrusting my dick further into my hand as I start to lose control. I cup her face then and she sighs. So fucking softly I can hardly hear it over my own pants, but I feel her exhale against my thumb resting along her bottom lip.

And that's when I know. As I ejaculate into my own hand, spurts of hot cum splashing over my abs and fist. My pulsing cock jerking in tempo with my turbulent heartbeat as I squeeze myself tighter and tighter in punishment. That I'm already gone. Obsession latches its filthy claws beneath my flesh and hooks in deep. A new sort of darkness rushing through my veins, depravity and madness weaving their way together and forcing themselves into my very bones.

I smile.

This girl is going to be my undoing.

CHAPTER 3
GRACE

Consciousness comes to me slowly. Inhaling a slow, deep breath, I stretch out my spine, uncurling my body like a feline in the sun. I huff out a soft breath, my fingers gently running over the soft cotton sheets, my skin wrapped in silk pyjamas. Everything so different to yesterday morning. I blink my eyes open, a little at a time, taking it easy to fully rouse from sleep. Swallowing down so many pills before bed can sometimes keep me groggy for hours. Only when they fully wear off do I really wake up. And then they're force feeding me more and the cycle starts again.

Early morning light streams in the huge window, my head turning to fully look out. The sun is still not really up yet, but the rain has cleared. I watch the heavens pass by for a short while, thin silver clouds drifting lazily across the sky, a pretty mixture of reds, purples and pinks as the sun climbs just a little higher. Shoving down the blankets, I swivel my feet over the edge of the big bed, my warm feet pressing against the cool wooden floor. I wriggle my toes, stretching out the arches of my feet. Wandering over to the window, my eyes diverting downward, I take in my new surroundings.

Trees of all kinds climbing their way into the heavens, the tops of them practically piercing through the wispy clouds. Bushes and shrubs, flowers and weeds alike cover the ground. A stream runs along the side of the house, disappearing from view as I crane my neck, my nose pressing against the glass, trying to see where it leads to. Small birds flitting between the trees, dropping down to the ground, hopping their way through the thicket. I watch for all movement, my eyes darting in all directions as I try to take it all in. My palms press hard against the windowpane, breath fogging the glass supporting my body as I struggle to get a closer look.

I want to be outside, the fresh air on my face, warm sun on my skin. How do I get down there?

I chew on my bottom lip, twitching from one foot to the other, I press away from the glass. Heading straight into the bathroom to relieve my bladder. I wash my hands, sweeping my fingers across the loose hairs in my face, tucking some fallen strands behind my ears. Rosie said these are called plaits, the things she knotted my hair into. I like it. I've never had anything done to my hair before, no one ever showing me how. Matron always pulled it back tightly in her fist when making me stare at myself in the mirror as punishment, usually after I'd been naughty or broken the rules. I knew better than to break the rules. After all, they were in place for a reason.

Like not looking Mother in the eye because mine are too strange. Knowing Mother's brutality when I accidently caught her gaze, her hazel eyes always flashing with anger when I did so. Or staying silent at school when strapped down at night. Both things in place to keep me safe. Only my disobedient behaviour and rule breaking made my days uncomfortable. If I did as I was instructed and not listen to the voice in my head then I was left alone.

Feeling those spikes again, I run my knuckles down the centre of my chest. Frowning when they don't go away. There has to be something in there. Some sort of creature inside me. I wonder how it got in here. Whatever it is is hurting me, as soon as I find something to cut it out with, I will. Staring down at my chest, I pinch my silky shirt, pulling the fabric away from my body so I can talk down to my skin.

"Whoever you are, just stay in there for a little while longer. I'll keep you safe until I can get you out."

Avoiding the bathroom mirror all together, I make my way straight to the bedroom door. I stand before it, my eyes boring into the wood, wishing I could see what was on the other side of it. I don't know who else lives in this house, who I'll run into if I exit my room without Rosie. Although, nobody said I wasn't allowed to leave my room and it wasn't locked last night. I haven't been given *any* rules yet. Perhaps I should just wait until someone comes to collect me, but I do really want to go outside.

Depressing the brass handle, my small fingers silently pulling the door towards me. I peek around it, a three-inch gap to investigate through, nothing but silence meeting my ears. The shadowed hallway I walked through last night looks the same, so I pull open the door. Closing it softly behind me as I enter the hall. My feet take on a mind of their own, carrying me quickly through the hall. I bypass all the closed doors, my eyes seeking out nothing but the stairs. The curved staircase comes into view, my feet carrying me down it, my hand gliding over the polished banister.

I wander through the first floor, drawn into darkness, the curtains closed, blocking out the early morning light. I drift through various rooms until I find a kitchen. Stone floors and cream walls, dark wooden cabinets and a large copper sink. The blinds in this room are open, a windowed door at the far end. I start to move quicker then, my heart thudding inside my chest as I get closer to the outside. I pull back the bolts that line the top and bottom of the door. Twisting the cast iron key in the handle lock. The key left there like anyone is welcome to leave. I wonder how true that might be for a moment, even as my fingers still fist the key, continuing to twist it open. It clicks, signalling its unlocked, I pause. Listening for any movement in the house. Half petrified that Mother could be behind me, half excited that the outside world is just within my reach. Hearing nothing, I pull open the door and sprint into the trees.

The toad I've been following croaks, long and low in its throat, its bumpy body leaping onto a rock at the edge of the stream. Another, some distance away, croaks back. Their deep calls have me venturing further into the marsh, up to my calves, my toes suctioning into the mud. The sun shines high in the sky, hidden from my view by the dense trees, but I can feel its warmth when the gentle wind blows, the leaves rustling and parting for the rays. Their thick, full branches casting the damp earth in shadow. I edge the shallow of the stream, the water babbling gently over rocks and pebbles that dig into the underside of my bare feet. A hare rushes past, birds singing high in the treetops, scuffles, snuffles and cawing keeps my ears buzzing with new sounds. Things I've never heard before. My toad plops himself into the water, disappearing from view and I feel my lips pout.

Turning away, I trudge my way through the mud. Travelling further into the trees, I dip low, brushing my fingers over wild flowers. Buttercups, crocuses, bluebells and lavender, all things I've seen in picture books. Collecting a daisy as I go, twirling the stalk between my finger and thumb I bring it to my nose, the tiny white petals tickling the tip. My bare feet sore, I rest my back against a tree, sliding down and dropping to my bum in the dirt. I sit still, quietly watching creatures and insects move around me. All so unaffected by my presence, none of them are warning me not to look at them. None of them calling me strange. Tucking the daisy into my braid, I listen to the bees buzz and the birds sing. A louder sound behind my tree catching my attention.

I whip my head over my shoulder, angling my body to peer around the trunk. The thick ferns hiding so much from my view, I push to my feet, wandering towards the sound that caught my attention. There, in the long grass, is a deer. It's smooth brown fur, a white nose and little white tail standing upright, large, bloated belly, too full and round to only be containing food. I crouch low, resting on my haunches, watching it graze. After a while, the deer raises its head, its ears pricked and twisting on the top of its head before darting off into the forest.

Looking up through the cover of trees, dark clouds roll over the sun, shadowing the earth from its rays. A shudder runs through me, goosebumps smattering my skin, a cold chill racing down my spine. The sky only does this when it's going to rain, one last glance in the direction the deer went. I decide I better turn back.

I spin around on my feet, all of the trees looking the same. Greens bleeding together, animal sounds filling my head, echoing around my skull. Unsure of which way to go I try to make my way back to the water.

Time passes me by, rain falling in sheets, soaking through my silk pyjamas. My feet aching, the arches pulling painfully with every step. Mud soaking my legs, my bottom uncomfortably wet from sitting in the damp grass. My tummy growls loudly, my insides grumbling with hunger. I keep walking forward, not knowing where I'm going, hoping I will recognise something. Nothing seems familiar, no tree or patch of flowers. And now the sky is dark, and the rain continues to fall, making my progress even slower. My feet squelch as they sink in the wet mud, and it takes extra effort to keep pulling my feet free. Just as I'm about to give up and find a hollow tree to perch inside of and rest my painful feet, a large dog springs into view.

I stop still.

My teeth chattering with cold now that I've stopped my tired muscles working. It's bellowing bark makes me jump, one short, loud, clipped sound. And another dog, the same, comes into view, stopping beside its buddy. They're not small in any sense of the word. Black shiny coats with dark brown markings along their faces, chests and bottom of their legs. Sharp pointed ears and short stubby tails. They both cock their heads, mimicking me as I do the same. I'm not frightened of them, but they're looking at me like I could be their next meal and I really don't think I could fight one off if it decided to pounce, let alone two. The rain is pelting down hard against my back now, the cover of trees not hindering the rainfall in the slightest. I shuffle half a step back, making both beasts bark at my attempted retreat. Their maw's dripping with saliva, teeth bared.

I turn to run, but as I twist, I smack headfirst into a firm chest. My legs buckle, stumbling. Huge hands reach out, gripping my upper arms and dragging me into him firmly, keeping me up on my feet. I squirm in his hold, his fingers pinching my skin as I try to break free. Blinking the rain free from my lashes, I look up at my stranger. His face is shadowed, half in the cover of darkness. The other half... the other half makes my heart thud, and my tummy knot, pins and needles race down my spine as my legs tremble. My teeth chattering coming to an abrupt halt as my lungs burn, breath caught in my throat.

A solid square jaw, sharp and angular, sun-kissed skin and deep, dark eyes. A thick mess of straight, jet-black hair atop his head, strong nose leading to dark, full lips. A white scar through his right brow, thin and shiny, jagged in shape, carving through the arch of dark hair.

He peers down at me, my gaze suddenly colliding with his, and it feels as though something hits me. Something strong and unforgiving smashes into my gut like a fist and my body wants to fall forward but the stranger still has hold of me. His grip tightening more on the tops of my arms, and it makes me wince, but it also doesn't feel like when Mother or Matron do it. The way his thick fingers cling onto me makes me feel safe somehow. Like even if the two beasts, that seem to have fallen silent now, were to lunge, he might shield me from them.

"Your eyes," he says.

The sound rough, deep, vibrating through his entire being, flowing freely into me through his hands on my arms. I tremble and I don't understand why, because I don't feel cold anymore, in fact, I don't seem to feel anything in this moment. Even the pain in my feet seems to have dissipated as though it were never really there to begin with.

I frown, quickly dropping my gaze to peer at the tops of my muddied toes. Remembering much too late that I shouldn't be looking people in the eye. I chew on my bottom lip, wondering what the punishment shall be for my rule-breaking. It's only my first day and I'm already going to be in trouble. My chin wobbles at the thought of Mother's reaction to my mess.

My stranger removes one of his hands from my arm, his thumb and finger pinching my trembling chin, he tilts my face up towards him. I keep my eyes averted, staring down so hard at the floor that I want to cry, and I don't know why, because I'm used to the punishments. The canings don't hurt me anymore and the beatings only leave temporary bruising. I know how to stay silent during, making the time spent on me less. They always like the weak ones. The emotional ones. The ones who cry out and beg and plead. That's why I don't do that anymore. I haven't made a sound during a correction since I was eight years old.

"Look at me."

Never one to disobey orders, my eyes snap up of their own accord, latching onto his dark brown ones. One still shadowed, one in perfect view. Chocolate brown with gold flecks like caramel, something lighter swirling around the centre, the outer ring so dark it's almost black. Perhaps it really is. I've never met anyone with eyes quite like his before.

"I always want you to look at me when I'm speaking to you," he murmurs, his rough voice commanding.

His fingers slide from their hold on my chin, knuckles sweeping across my jawbone, goosebumps razing over my skin like fire. Everything inside me tenses, unsure how he heard my thoughts. I flutter my lashes, desperately trying to stop tears mixing with the raindrops already cascading down my face. I stare into his eyes and everything around me just seems to fall away.

"Your eyes are so beautiful," my stranger tells me, but he doesn't smile. "They're wasted locked on the ground," that heavy rumble thrumming through his chest.

My heart squeezes at his words, and I suddenly remember the creature trapped inside there. But I can't think too much about it right now, he said my eyes are beautiful. Not *strange*, not weird, not frightening or disturbing.

Beautiful.

His words make warmth flush through my veins, my fingers tremble by my sides and I realise I should be scared. Lost in the dark woods with a stranger. But I don't feel scared. I don't feel scared at all. I feel warm, like the sun is on my skin even though it's not and I'm pretty sure it's nighttime now. And I don't feel lonely. I'm not alone and this man will keep me safe.

And I'm wondering how I could know these things. Because I don't *think* he'll keep me safe, something in his gaze *tells* me he will. This isn't what normal girls would think in the company of a stranger, Mother would say, but in this moment, I suddenly like being strange. I peek up into his eyes again, his thumb smoothing the damp skin beneath my eye.

"I'm going to take you home now, Grace."

My name on his tongue makes me want to weep. The way he says it, no malice or anger. It's just my name, nothing more and nothing less. And yet, it already feels like so much.

He slides his huge hand down my arm, loosening his grip on me and taking my hand instead. I look down at our joint hands, mine tiny in comparison to his huge one folded around mine. I look back up at him, opening my mouth to speak. To tell him I'm not supposed to talk to strangers, let alone hold hands with one. When it occurs to me, I haven't actually *spoken* to him at all.

CHAPTER 4
HUNTER

Dad came home with Thorne, they were on a job when Eleanor called him, supposedly hysterical at losing her daughter... I'm not sure I've ever been more tempted to roll my eyes in all my life.

Dad sent me out to find her. Thorne offered to help. I growled and told him no. He smirked, I panicked, promptly got the dogs and left without another word.

After they explained that Eleanor's missing daughter was in fact this tiny, frail girl with moonlit skin and too much gold hair. My new *stepsister*. I almost had a visible reaction at that little piece of information. I knew Eleanor had a daughter. A girl locked away for her *'unusual manner and disgracing behaviour'*. A girl with *problems*. That's what that bitch said to my father. He wanted her to live here with us. Eleanor didn't. I didn't care either way. But now, I think, perhaps I might.

I think of how I slept last night. For the first time in

my life, I slept soundly. I didn't toss or turn after what I did. I felt, well, I felt *something* and I'm not sure I've ever really felt anything before.

Until her.

I look down between our bodies. My tall, lean one, thin but stacked with hard packed muscle from riding the horses, running the dogs and moving the corpses. Her skinny frame, cloaked in hair with big, round eyes. One an enchanting, ice blue, the other a warm hazel, much like her mother's, but also not. Eleanor's are always burning with rage, her temper simmering just beneath the surface. Not that Dad notices. That, or he just doesn't care. Thorne always liked the angry ones too. Perhaps it's a Blackwell thing. Maybe just a man thing. Grace's eye doesn't have that. In its place, something much worse. Nothingness. Cold and dead. Unseeing.

I glance at our hands, my huge one smothering her small. She didn't try to draw away from me. Didn't ask me who I was. There was no *stranger danger* alarm going off inside that pretty little head. She just looked up at me. Her delicate neck craning back, arching like it would, should my knuckles find themselves fisted in her hair. One of her thick braids frayed apart, wide chunks of hair loose, leaves and twigs matted through the rest. Skin so pale and perfect. Blemish free.

I force myself to look away.

Tyson and Duke trot up ahead, both dogs knowing the way home as easily as I. I watch her from the corner of my eye as we walk. She doesn't seem to be afraid at all. Not even a little unsure. She just lets me lead and I hate it because it feels too natural. Like we've been destined to be this way together forever. Something written in the stars. But when I glance at her again, not able to stop myself. Hoping to catch sight of her beautiful eyes on me, my own fall to her soaked pyjamas.

The white silk now translucent, the rain sticking them to her creamy, smooth skin. Even in the dark I can see her small nipples, arrowed into sharp points, tenting the wet fabric. I bite my lip, swallowing hard, shooting my eyes forward. Willing my painfully hard dick to go back down. I knew I'd fucked up last night. Breaking the cycle. I've never wanted to touch myself before. Not for me, not over anyone else. I just don't get aroused. I don't feel anything. But one night. One moment of weakness. One uncontrollable lapse in judgement and I'm like a fifteen-year-old boy all over again. Well, technically speaking. I never actually did those things as a teenager either… but still. I'm a grown fucking man, I need to get some goddamn self-control.

I clench my jaw, my fingers tightening around hers, but she doesn't even flinch. I can feel her bones grind together beneath my grip, yet she elicits nothing. No wince, no blinking, no squirming in my hold. No, if anything, her grip tightens on me right back. Like she *wants* me to be holding onto her. I've never been good at reading people's reactions but even I know hers are not *normal.*

Her large eyes locked forward, wet hair plastered to her pale forehead, small puffs of breath escaping her parted lips. She walks with me blindly. Totally at ease and it makes me grow tenser. What is wrong with this girl? Why is she not trying to scrabble away from me? What is so dysfunctional inside her skull that she would take leave with a stranger, three times her size, whether she were lost or not. This isn't a normal reaction.

It's *strange*.

The dogs continue bounding forward, my brow pulled down in a frown, teeth clenching as I grind my jaw. Anger courses through my veins, white hot rage bubbling like witches brew just beneath the surface. Frustrated that she would be so reckless. Maybe the girl is mute. Perhaps she doesn't function fully. She's been locked away from society for the last twelve years.

In a *school*.

I didn't mean to do it.

I just needed to see how it worked.

My older brother Wolf told me all about its insides and I just wanted to see.

It was an accident.

I was curious.

Mum was frightened.

Our oldest brother Thorne shouted at her when she screamed at me.

But now I'm here.

Archer said he'd call Dad.

But I'm still stuck here.

. . .

Thunder claps overhead, shaking me free from my memories. The rain that had started to slow, picks back up. Grace shivers, the tremble in her hand ricocheting up my arm, humming in my shoulder. Everything in me warms, liking the feel of her arm brushing against mine as we walk, her cold fingers inside my warm palm. Reluctantly releasing her hand, I strip off my jacket. Draping it over her slim shoulders, she watches me all the while. I can feel her gaze locked on me. On my every tiny movement. Her eyes flicking around in their sockets.

She's tracking me.

I almost smile, but I don't. Quickly stopping myself feeling anything around her. I don't understand how she provokes these reactions out of me. My family haven't been able to coax even a simple eye roll out of me my entire life. So what's so special about this slight of a girl? Barely a woman, turned eighteen only a few days ago. The girl knows nothing. And if she knew what it was I did every day inside of the mill, she certainly wouldn't be holding onto my hand like she'll never let go. Not willingly anyway.

I grab for her hand again, tugging her sharply along behind me when she doesn't immediately move. She stumbles, but I don't care. I need to get back. I have things to do.

I drag her behind me, nothing but silence from her. Irritation spikes inside me, my blood boiling. Speak! Just say fucking something. Jesus H Christ. I want her to tell me to slow down. Cry out as her bare toes bash into exposed tree roots and the torn soles of her feet trample over thistles. But she doesn't do any of those things. Even when I pull her arm so hard I hear her shoulder joint crack. She just stumbles along behind me. Her grip *tightening* like she wants to be attached to me. And it fucks me up.

I'm fucked up.

I tear her through the marsh, squeezing her bony knuckles. Hauling her along behind me, she says nothing. Freezing rain soaking us both, the Dobermans leaping through the wildflowers, yipping up ahead as they bound toward the stables. My booted feet meet the cobbled path. I spin, yanking her against my chest, her chin hitting my sternum. The breath rushing out of her lungs as my jacket drops to the floor with a splat. She peers up at me, the light from the stable door illuminating her creamy skin and my fingers itch to slice into it. To watch hot crimson flow down her throat, roll over her breasts and flat belly. Dripping down to the V between her legs.

My fists suddenly grasp either side of her silk pyjama shirt, and I'm point-three seconds away from tearing through the buttons. My heavy breathing panting through my nostrils like a demonic bull. I glance at her face, her mismatched eyes bore into my own, her chin wobbling, and I freeze. Staring down at her, only my grip on her shirt holding her up, her toes grazing the ground as I support her weight. She keeps looking at me. Unblinking. I can't release my fingers; I can't bring myself to stop touching her. My insides twist, my lower belly knotting and warming all at the same time. I clench my teeth, squeezing my eyes closed. Desperately trying to claw my way back to earth when something brushes my cheek.

My eyes snap open, Grace's large orbs still locked on mine. Her fingers glide over my cheekbone, cool and damp, her skin smells like earth. I pull in a sharp breath, her fingertips continuing to ghost over my face as I slowly lower her feet to the floor. Sucking in lungful after lungful of her scent. The rain and wildflowers have tinted her natural smell, but it's there. Something underneath all the mud and daisies.

My upper body bends with her descent to the ground. Instantly crowding her as she touches down, I back her up into the side of the stable, her touch still on my face. I grip her hips, my thumbs pressing harshly into her, her back thumps into the wooden stall. Her head hits next, a resounding thud, but she doesn't wince. She doesn't blink. Her gaze firmly focused on me.

Only me.

Don't stop looking at me, baby girl.

My breathing gets heavier, my dick gets harder and everything inside of me screams to get away from her, but instead, I lean in. Water from my dark hair sluices over my face, dripping onto her mouth as I touch my forehead to hers. Raindrops gather on her pouty bottom lip, rolling over as they gather, falling down her chin. I breathe against her. My hips pinning hers, every hard inch of me smothers her, but still, she doesn't object. Her delicate fingers continue to touch my face. Despite our closeness, she explores my features. My eyes closed, her fingertips ghost over my eyelids, trace down my nose, up my cheekbone and along my jaw. My heart thuds so hard in my chest it feels like it's trying to break free. But hers remains calm, her heartbeats paced and even. Her breathing slow and controlled, despite having a bloodthirsty beast looming over her. A hard cock thrust tight against her lower belly.

My thumbs dig in deeper, her bony hips carving into the webbing between my fingers and thumb. Sharp and protruding. Smoothing my thumbs up and down, gently moving them beneath the hem of her shirt. My breathing so erratic I can hardly think straight. I just need to touch her skin. That's all. Just one little touch and I'll get over it. Whatever *it* is.

I push my body harder against hers, my solid form crushing her frail one. The coarse pads of my thumbs finally slip beneath her top, snagging against her velvety flesh, she gasps against the shell of my ear. Her fingers suddenly fisting in my hair, twisting the strands, tearing at the root so hard I come. My pulsing cock thrusts against her as I come and come in my tight jeans, and it feels like it'll never fucking end as her nails scrape against my scalp. The lengths of my hair pulled tight against my head, her knuckles cracking as she tightens her hold, continuing to yank.

Collapsing onto her, I lean my forehead against the wood panelling of the stable. My fingers smoothing up, beneath her shirt, hands cinching her tiny waist. Her heart bangs against her breastbone now, her breathing, too, uncontrolled. Her hand moves down, smoothing over my hair, latching around my bicep instead, her hold delicate.

Catching my breath, I push back. Looking down at her, those contrasting eyes still locked on me. I flex my fingers on her waist, feeling her supple skin beneath my calloused palms. My large hands almost touching around her middle. Her tiny frame trembles, her teeth chattering slightly. Ignoring the mess in my boxers, I grip her hand, leading her back to the house.

CHAPTER 5

GRACE

I sit at the kitchen table. A plastic floral tablecloth covering the wood beneath. Rosie stands off to the left, her small round body resting back against the brass sink. Stryder stands to the right, his smart trousers and shirt making me feel underdressed. I am, after all, in my nightclothes. Another man stands beside him. Tall and dark with those same brown eyes. Perhaps Stryder's brother? Son?

I stare down at my lap, my fingers knotted together. Mud and leaves stain my silky white pyjamas. I knew Mother would be upset. I just really wanted to be outside. My tummy growls again and I purse my lips, knowing there is absolutely no way I'll be fed tonight. Not after what I did. Running out of the house, into the woods. A man having to spend time finding me.

He disappeared once he seated me at the table. Leaving me without another word. His behaviour wild and erratic, calm and gentle to aggressive and impatient.

But I liked it all. His softness when he first held my hand, his pretty face and sharp jaw. Those big brown eyes that saw me. He knew my name but didn't give me his.

"What did you think you were doing?" Mother snaps, banging a hand down on the table.

I hold my breath, keeping my eyes on my dirt filled nails. Not answering.

"Grace!"

Her shrill voice makes me shiver, I gnaw on my lips, the top then the bottom. Repeating the motion as she taps her foot on the stone floor. That feeling jerks inside my chest again and I swallow hard against it, not knowing what to do.

"Well? What were you doing out there, Grace?" she snaps again, and I squeeze my eyes shut tight. "Answer me right now, young lady or you're going straight back to the academy!"

Academy.

I shift in my wooden chair, my thigh bones digging into it uncomfortably. It's a very hard chair. I thought people that lived in big houses had nice things. I would have at least expected there to be cushions.

"Grace!" she screeches, finally exasperated with my silence.

I'm not trying to be rude; I just don't know what I'm supposed to be doing whilst I'm here. Nobody's told me the rules.

"I just wanted to see outside," I reply quietly, gaze

still caught on my knuckles. "I wasn't locked inside, so…" I trail off, my brow pulling taut.

"This is completely unacceptable behaviour, Grace. Your disappearance has ruined everyone's day! Stryder had to waste his time and energy coming home from his busy workday because you were missing. He then had to pull your stepbrothers away from their jobs to go and look for you. You are wasting everybody's time here, we're all very busy people. What if Hunter hadn't found you at all? What would you have done then, hmm? You need to stay inside your room and find something to do with yourself, Grace. No more trouble making. You are not to wander. At all. Do you understand me?" Mother scolds and it's so much worse hearing it come from her instead of Matron.

I blink my eyes rapidly, hot liquid burning at the back of them, nodding my head once.

"I told you this was a bad idea, Stryder. She should not be here! She needs locking away with people like her. It's dangerous for her to be wandering freely around the house."

Mother continues as though I'm not here at all, but I tune out the rest, not needing to hear her call me strange. I continue sitting in the hard wooden chair, a small pool of water steadily growing beneath my feet. Mothers voice still echoing around me, Stryder's deep rumble interjecting every so often. I hear none of it though.

Instead, I stay locked inside my head.

Thinking about my stranger.

Hunter.

That's his name.

The man who found me.

Hearing his name makes moths flutter around inside my tummy. Hunter came to search for me, he told me my eyes were beautiful. He held my hand, let me touch his face, and then, *he did something else.* He liked it when I hurt him back. And then he was soft with me again. I could feel his eyes on me even when I wasn't looking. He said he always wanted me to look at him when he spoke to me.

Does that mean he'll do it again?

No one ever talks to me. And I like how he sounds. He had such a deep voice; I felt his words all the way down to my bones.

"Grace?"

"Yes?" I reply in a low voice, knowing it's Stryder that's addressing me.

"You can look at me, sweetheart," he prompts gently.

My neck hesitating to lift, I glance up, my head bowed, eyeballs flicking to the tops of my eyelids. His dark eyes warm when I look at him, a small smile curving his lips.

"What can I do to make you happy living here?" he asks me as quietly as he spoke before.

He drops down into a crouch beside me, I hear Mother scoff. I swallow hard. Not knowing how to answer. Happy? Living here?

"I just want you to enjoy living here with us, with

me, your stepbrother. I want you to be comfortable. What is it you enjoy doing with your time, Grace?" such a comforting man, the polar opposite of Mother.

I wonder why he married her.

"I-" stopping myself, I swallow past the tightness in my throat.

Trying to predict the right answer, I struggle. What is it he wants me to say?

"You can tell me, Grace, whatever it is, if it's within my power I'll do it, or get it for you. Whatever you say, there are no wrong answers," I glance up at him again, trying to get a read on his face.

His words feel genuine, but I don't know this man. My new stepfather. Perhaps he is very good at playing pretend. Stryder's dark eyes crinkle at the outer corners as he smiles at me. Mother attempts to say something, Stryder twisting sharply, shutting her up without a word.

"I want to know what the rules are," I utter gently, hoping I'm not scolded for speaking out of turn.

We have company and it's hard to know whether Stryder really wants me to speak freely, or if it's just a good show put on for the other man in the kitchen.

"The rules?" Stryder repeats after a moment, my words echoed back to me as a question. His dark brows knitting together on his forehead. "There are no *rules* here, Grace. This is your home. You can do as you please. Well, within reason of course, no indoor bonfires," he chuckles lightly, making me frown harder, my bottom lip pouting.

Why would anyone have a bonfire inside?

"Dad," the other man calls, answering my question about their relationship.

Stryder glances over his shoulder, before looking back at me. His smile broadens and I hold my breath.

"The only rules here, Grace," he says, holding up his curled fist. "Are to explore," a finger shoots up, "enjoy yourself," another finger joining the first. "And learn everything you can about Heron Mill. We have acres and acres of land to explore, all of my sons constantly flit in and out, they'll all be happy to show you the groun-"

"All of?" I question, interrupting, Stryder's words stopping short.

My cheeks heat, gaze dropping.

"Yes," he chuckles again, the sound carefree and light. "*All* of. I have six sons, so technically you have six big brothers to pester to your heart's content." He turns away again, still in a crouch position before me, his forearms resting on his bent knees. "This is your oldest step-brother Thorne," he introduces, my eyes lifting once more, taking another quick look at the man that was previously standing behind Mother.

Thorne's moved closer now, stood just behind his father. Black swirls decorate his olive complexion, licks of it peeking out of his shirt collar and rolled cuffs. Deep black hair, wavy like his fathers, is cut short on his head. His dark brown eyes have that familiar shimmer of gold running through them, *like Hunter's*. He smiles just slightly, but it doesn't look natural. I quickly glance back down at my hands.

"Then there's Wolf, Archer, Arrow and Raine. You'll meet them as they come and go. None of them live here now, but they stop by frequently, they all still work for various areas of the family business. And of course, you've already met my middle boy Hunter, I trust he was kind when he found you."

Hunter.

I lick my lips, tasting the rain, and it makes me think of him even more. Raindrops fell from his face, landing onto mine. I tasted the water from his tanned skin, swallowing down a little piece of his essence. He smelled like the forest. Like wet moss, daisies and the babbling brook. His body towering over me, my back grazing against the wood panelling as he thrust himself against me.

Nobody's ever held me like that before.

Like they didn't want to let go.

Couldn't.

I nod my head. My answer seemingly enough to please my new stepfather. He rises from his crouch, jerking his head at his son. Thorne leaves the room, I stay seated in my chair, Stryder speaking quietly in Mother's ear. I can feel her watchful gaze, her evil hazel eyes burning a hole through my skull. My eyes averted still, I feel the weight of her stare as the room empties, no one but her and I remain.

She waits then, pausing to listen as the footsteps get further and further away and the voices drop into silence. Then she's springing into action. Her nails carve into my arm as she drags me up out of the chair, pain shooting up my calves as she forces me to stand on my cut feet. She shakes me, her hand locked around my bicep, grip intense.

"You think you can turn up here and ruin my life?" she spits. "You're a sick, *sick* girl, Grace. Making moon eyes at *my* husband, you little bitch," she hisses. "I saw you, the way you *looked* at him. I'll kill you before you get your poisonous hooks in him. I can make you disappear into that forest you seem to love so much, making sure no one will ever find your body. Do you understand me, little girl? *I* am in charge here, not you, not your step-daddy. *Me*."

She shakes me again, my brain rattling around inside my skull, before she slams me back down into the chair. The front two feet lifting off the ground as my weight topples into it. I watch the bones in the tops of my feet flex, my bleeding toes curling into the cold floor as the chair slams down.

"You will not fuck this up for me, Grace. If you do, it'll be the biggest mistake of your life so far, do you understand?"

I nod silently, wishing I was anywhere but here. The back of her hand cracks across my cheek. My head whipping to the side, pain bolting along my jaw, my ear pounding with pain, heartbeat thudding in the pit of my stomach. My hair flies over my face, strands sticking to my split lip, a trickle of blood running down my chin. Cheek burning like lava, my head still slung to the side, I lick my lips, tasting copper.

"It ends now, no more wandering. If I find out

you've left your room without a chaperone, you'll regret it. Mark my words, Grace."

And with that departing promise, she stalks from the room, her clacking heels echoing down the hall, like an ominous death knell.

CHAPTER 6

HUNTER

I pace my room, tearing off my drenched clothes. Footsteps heavy, the corner lamp switched on, dimmed. Tyson and Duke watch from their place on the bed as I work my way back and forth across the cold floor. Hands running through my hair, I tear at the strands, fisting at the root.

Not the way she did it.

I squeeze my eyes shut tightly. Frustration rushes through my veins, my naked skin smelling of *her*. Like honeysuckle and ferns, sweet, a woodsy undercurrent. Something that makes my skin tingle, and my dick irritatingly hard. My control is an electrical cable, a frayed wire, worn down quickly because of too much current pulsing through it. If it snaps...

If it snaps.

"Fuck!"

My fist slams into the wall, knuckles impacting with the solid surface, there's no give in the old stone. Skin splitting, knuckles continuing to pummel into the wall. My left hand splayed over my head as I pound my right fist into the limestone over and over. Dropping my forehead forward, I slap my bleeding hand flat against the wall. Resting my weight on my head, my breath heaving through my lungs.

I left her there.

Threw her to the wolves, she sat at that goddamn kitchen table, those wide, mismatched eyes tracking me as I made my way around the kitchen, avoiding her gaze. She wanted me to look at her. To stay. To say something. To do anything. *Be* there. *For her.*

Disgusted.

That's what I am.

With myself.

With this *infatuation.*

Never has anything gotten beneath my skin like this. *Anyone.*

Hooked claws with toxic secretions, her sweet poison travelling towards my heart. And I'm not sure I don't like it.

That innocent face, her silence, the way she didn't stop me. Didn't tell me no. She wanted to be there too.

Like she knew she was mine.

One night, she's been inside this house for one night and my brain is about ready to explode. A white-hot poker searing me straight through the chest, like I fell on my own fucking blade and didn't even realise what was happening until it was too late. The feeling giving me a high like I've never experienced before.

Pushing off the wall, I grab a pair of grey jogging bottoms, cuffed at the ankles, and pull them on. Wiping my split knuckles down the leg, I flop backwards onto the bed, the thick, brown fur throw soft against my goosebump pricked flesh. Both dogs shift closer, curling themselves into one another, their large, lean bodies lying beside me warms my damp skin like a furnace. I drop my forearm across my face, pressing against my hot eyelids. I inhale, a long, slow breath, meant to calm my racing heart, but I catch that scent again.

It's barely there, sweet and subtle, but it's all I can smell now. Ferns and honeysuckle and rain. It's scary how I can so easily differentiate between my rain soaked skin and hers. The floral cutting through it like a sharp, bitter tang of lemon. I grit my teeth, grinding my jaw as my softening dick starts to harden once more. I'm completely out of control and knowing how close she is…

Grace.

She'll be back in her room by now. Two floors above me, only sixteen rooms between her soft, supple body and mine. I sit up, swinging my legs over the side of the wooden bedframe, toes pressed to the floor. Tilting my head back, my eyes boring into the ceiling like I could see her if I stare hard enough. I sigh, rolling my neck on my tense shoulders.

Don't do it.

Do not go up there. I don't need to see her. She's meant to be my new fucking *sister*, for Christ's sake. It couldn't be any more wrong than it already is. Than what I've already done. I stand up, storming across my room, my fist tight on the handle, a low whine in protest from Tyson hits my ears. I throw a look over my shoulder, both boys staring at me with tilted heads. I flex my fingers on the brass, knowing I should stay here, and push the door open.

I'm outside her room again. Ear pressed flush to the wood, palms flat against the smooth door. My chest heaving with uncontrolled breaths, eyes squeezed shut tight, I let myself in. Moonlight streams in from the large window, falling across the dark interior, my eyes flicking straight to the bed. It's made, uncrumpled sheets perfectly folded back, but nobody is inside it. I take a few steps further inside, the bathroom door is cracked open, darkness beyond it. I stand at the end of the bed, my fingers curling over the carved wooden footboard.

Her tiny body is curled in tight, face pressed against the glass of the window. Arms wrapped around her knobbly knees, drawn up to her chin. A white nightdress smothers her like a sheet, disguising her as the ghost she probably thinks she is. I step closer, she doesn't look up, doesn't move, doesn't speak.

I crouch down before her, my fingers slowly reaching across, brushing the thick golden hair off her face, it's damp, not from the shower. She smells like rain still. She shudders, the only tell-tale sign of life. Her beautiful eyes still locked on the view beyond the window.

Look at me.

I shift onto my arse, elbows atop my bent knees. Less than a foot between us, she continues staring out the window, I continue staring at her. The moon washing over her ice white skin makes her glow like a divine spirit. Her golden hair like an oversized halo surrounding her bony body. I look out to my right, my dark eyes taking in the swaying trees, the soft patter of rain tapping against the glass. I think of dragging her back out there, pulling her through the marsh, forcing her into the pond. Her wet skin slipping and sliding against mine.

I bite the inside of my cheek. I've never wanted to do any of these things before and now I'm thinking about doing them to my new stepsister. The one I hardly knew existed.

Did she know about me?

"Grace?" I say quietly, unable to stop myself.

Needing to hear her voice.

She looks down at the ground below, her large eyes anywhere but on me. Heat licks at my skin, my hand snapping out, I grip her chin, sharply tugging her face towards me.

"What did I tell you about looking at me when I'm speaking to you, Grace?" I bite out, her eyes still frustratingly averted.

I close my own, breathing out through my nose, my thumb pressing hard into her chin. The knuckle of my bent finger digging into the soft hollow beneath. I sigh quietly, loosening my hold.

"Look at me, Grace," I murmur softly, and I feel her inhale, exhale, her warm breath feathering over the back of my hand. "I'm Hunter," I tell her. "I would really like it if you would look at me, Grace," I coo gently, trying to coax her into trusting me.

She shouldn't.

But I'd like her to.

I'm going to hurt her.

Slowly. Very slowly. She rolls her eyes upward, her thick flare of dark lashes fanning out, the tips of them touching her blonde brows. The dark freckle beneath her hazel eye, harsh against her pale skin. I thumb her bottom lip, frowning.

"Who hurt you?" I ask, the coarse pad of my thumb ghosting over her newly split lip.

I look up into her eyes, the one I know to be ice blue, hidden behind her drape of hair. Her hazel eye studies me. Her chin wobbles, I shift closer. Encroaching on the very little personal space I originally left between us. I widen my thighs, flattening my legs to the floor, sliding forward until she's between my thighs. My hand slides along her jaw, turning her head towards me more, away from the window. I tuck her hair behind her ear, easing it back, curling it around. A fading handprint, three very visible finger marks. I grind my teeth, my jaw cracking under the pressure, I suck in a short, sharp breath.

"Tell me who hit you, Grace," I order softly, never having to use such a tender tone before. "Just tell me," I whisper, already knowing the answer.

Eleanor.

Bet Dad doesn't know the bitch hits her daughter.

My thick fingers flare across her heated cheek, smothering the burning handprint with my own. I stare at my tanned skin, harsh against her pale, I spend a lot of time in the sun. On my horses, with the dogs, walking and running. My thumb caresses the apple of her cheek, I watch mesmerised as it moves delicately across her warm flesh.

"I want you to talk to me, Gracie," I say mindlessly, gaze still focused on the movement of my thumb. "I want to hear your words. Listen to how your tongue rolls with R's and hisses with S's, watch your lips pout and purse."

I swallow, my eyes finally shooting back to hers. Her gaze on me now, my face mere inches from hers. Who leant in closer and when is a complete mystery to me, but I feel her breath on my face. Smell her sweet skin, her swollen, split bottom lip parted from the top. My eyes drop closed, I breathe her in, her scent overwhelming all of my senses. Touching our foreheads together, oxygen passing from my lungs into hers. I'm in her space, consuming it, eradicating everything that's not me. Everything about me unavoidable. I fill her vision, her nostrils, my air forces itself into her lungs. I rub my forehead against hers. Marking her face with my scent, running my nose down the length of hers. Breathing her in as I go, stopping as my lips reach hers. They don't touch, but they could.

If I wanted them to.

I've never kissed anyone before.

I've never wanted to.

I don't know if I want to try now.

Instead, I lay my cheek against her sore one,

absorbing the heat from the sting into my own flesh. Absolving her of her pain. I ghost my lips lightly to the place on her cheek just before her ear. She gasps almost silently against the shell of my own, and I feel a small smile curve one corner of my lips.

"What do you sound like when you're not gasping in my ear, baby girl?" I whisper into the dark, my lips brushing her lobe.

My other hand comes up, smoothing over her thick hair, cradling the crown of her head in my palm. I lean back slightly, my lips stopping just before hers again, and look into her eyes. Hers flicker, her attention solely on me.

"Tell me who hit you, little sister." She drops her gaze. "Nu-uh, eyes on me, baby girl." Obediently her eyes draw up, I hide my smirk. "Whisper their name into the darkness."

She licks her lips, her throat working as she swallows, and my dick grows firmer. She must be able to feel it through my thin joggers, pressing against her shin, her legs drawn up into her body resting between my spread thighs. I stroke her hair, letting the glossy, damp strands slide between my fingers like silk ribbons.

"*Hunter*," she whispers, and I groan.

Her voice like *nothing* I have ever heard before. Every letter dropping from her tongue has me enraptured. The soft lilt in her tone, like attempting to say one harsh word could snap her very vocal cords. Euphonic. Her voice is as gentle and as beautiful as she is.

Fragile.

So easily broken.

Her weakness calls to me like a wounded rabbit to a fox. Bleeding and limping and just *praying* to have its neck snapped by sharp teeth.

My grip tightens on her hair, I watch her watching me, my fingers twisting at the root, I tug her forward, our heads almost colliding.

"Say my name like that again, baby girl, and I won't be able to stop myself from hurting you," I growl, my deep voice low, breathing shallow.

She watches me as though deciding her fate, and I chuckle, a rough demonic sound spilling like venom from my throat.

"I'm a killer, Gracie," I tell her softly now, such a sharp contrast to my words before. "How does that make you feel, knowing your big brother could hurt you when he's supposed to protect you?"

I push a strand of hair behind her ear with my other hand, my split knuckles grazing across her pale, moonlit skin. A sticky smear of crimson left in my wake, I roll my knuckles back across her skin, marking her cheekbone with my essence. My breathing picks up, heart lurching, heaving in my chest like it's trying to escape out of my throat.

"Everybody hurts me," she whispers vulnerably.

My eyes snap to hers, searching, *hoping* to see the lie. Her wide eyes suck me in, glossy with tears and my dick only grows harder. I'm so hard it fucking *hurts*. And I realise it's because *I* want to be the one to hurt her.

The *only* one.

I swallow hard, my Adam's apple bobbing in my throat. Buzzing rushes through my ears as I drag her up by the fist in her hair. She doesn't fight me. Her feet scramble beneath her, struggling to make purchase as I haul her across the room. Her hands don't come up to her hair though, she doesn't try to cling onto me, pry my fingers away, gouge her nails into the back of my hand. No. She leans into it, moving with me as much as she can with our height and size difference. Spinning her in my hold, I rush her, the backs of her legs hitting the edge of the mattress. She falls, I fall with her, crushing her beneath my weight, the breath rushes out of her. Body tangled up in her long nightgown, it acts as a restraint, helping to pin her frail skeleton beneath me.

I dip my head, my nose to her hair, I breathe her in. Her chest heaving, I can hear her heart thudding against her breastbone, the sound drives me wild. My body strung tight with adrenaline, my steel cock pressing angrily against the inside of her thigh. I suck in a breath between my teeth. Hissing as she attempts to shift beneath me, warmth from her core flooding into me.

I tug her up by the hair, her neck arching painfully. I drag her into me, her chest brushing mine with ragged, uncontrolled breaths. My other hand slides up her night-dress, delicately smoothing my way up the outside of her thigh. Goosebumps prickle her flesh, my touch razing its way across her supple skin. I pant against her, our noses touching, she continues to stare into my eyes. I grind myself against her leg, my painfully hard dick desperately trying to rip free. My fingers in her hair so tight I can feel strands around my knuckles, snapping free from her scalp. My hand grazes the top of her thigh, the crease in her bent leg between thigh and hip. I freeze, finding nothing but bare skin, my hand stalled, desperate to creep further.

"Where is your underwear, little sister?" I hush against her lips, mine caressing hers with every word.

She licks her lips, the tip of her tongue *just* touching my mouth as it darts out.

"They were wet," she whispers, a tremble in her chest that makes me want to grin.

"Uh-huh," I raise a brow, a smirk playing on my lips. "Wet?" I question. "Why were your knickers wet, Gracie?" My words mocking but dead, not enough emotion in my voice to fully tease her.

"From the pond," she whispers again, the lullaby softness caressing my soul.

"Is that *all* they were wet from?"

She shivers in my hold, my fingers digging into her flesh, my thumb sliding back and forth down that crease on the inside of her thigh. She nods, her eyes dropped, she sucks in a sharp breath.

"Are you *lying* to me?" I tut sharply. "Blackwells don't tell lies, which means baby sisters don't tell lies either. You're a Blackwell now, Grace," I inform her, my fist in her hair not loosening, despite the strands of hair tearing from her head. "Now, tell me, baby girl. If I slide my hand down just a *tiny* bit further," emphasising my words by dragging my thumb an inch lower. "Will I find you wet?" I swallow as she shakes. "*For me?*"

She heaves in a sharp, shallow breath, wincing at the pull of her roots. She attempts to shake her head, my thumb pressing into her soft flesh so hard I know it'll bruise.

"Don't lie," I hiss through my teeth. "You're too beautiful to lie," I whisper the confession, my thumb moving lower despite her denial.

The heat from her cunt radiating towards my fist like a homing beacon I want nothing more than to sink my thick digits into.

"*Hunter*," she whispers, a half moan, half plea, that has my eyes rolling into the back of my head.

The power I wield over her in this moment, knowing I could do anything I wanted, and no one would stop me. She wouldn't stop me. No one else is on this floor of the house. No one would hear her scream.

I drag my hand out from her skirt, rising up on my haunches, my fist in her hair tearing free. Thick golden strands woven around my fingers; she flops to the bed. Gasping for breath, her eyes still locked on mine. I stand, my bare feet backing me away from her. Lifting up on her elbows she watches me, tracking me, once again, across the cold wooden floor. My back slams into the wall, my hand moving behind me, desperately clawing for the handle. I wrench it open, back myself into the darkened hallway and slam the door shut on her.

CHAPTER 7
GRACE

I wade through the marsh, the thick sludge cool against my scraped feet. The mud oozing its way between my bare toes, a light drizzle mists the air. I've been here for just over two weeks now and I haven't seen Hunter again. The creature inside my chest claws at me when I think of him. Stryder told me he sent Hunter on a job with his brothers, something for a family friend, he wouldn't tell me what though. Mother scolded me for being nosey, Stryder chuckled and encouraged my *'refreshing curiosity'*.

So many conflicting rules.

After that night in my room, when Hunter ran away from me. He *hurt* me, but I... It felt good when he did it, the *way* he did it. It wasn't like when Matron pulled my hair or caned me. It wasn't like Mother's hand leaving a sting upon my cheek. I brush the back of my hand across my forehead, pushing my hair back from my damp skin. I've been trying to learn a route. Trees, rocks, streams, ponds and the lake. All things to help me make my way back to the mill. Despite Mother's threats to lock me up in my room, I've been wandering the woods every day. Come rain or shine, here is where I've been.

My ears prick up, a rustle to my right claiming my attention. I take a few soft steps across the wildflower spotted grass. Red poppies, tiny pink and blue flowers scattered through the long grass. I dip down low, my footsteps slow, my fingers sweeping through the meadow floor, I clutch a handful of daisies. Scooping them into my fist, separating the rogue blades of grass, dropping them to the forest floor. Holding my bunch of daisies, I make my way silently towards the sound that claimed my attention. A louder rustle hits my ears, and I spot the deer I've been watching the last couple of weeks. Only, her belly isn't round anymore. She stands proudly in the tall brush, a tiny fawn at her feet.

I sink to my knees in the dirt, placing aside my daisies, my white cotton dress instantly soaking up moisture from the earth. The doe washes her baby, her tongue lapping at the sticky mess coating the baby's red-brown fur, a fluffy upturned tail, back speckled with white. I watch from my position in the ferns as the mother tends to her kid, the fawn wobbly on her new legs. The rain patters down, the drops gentle, refreshingly cool in the warm air, but still enough to soak through my hair. Water runs down my face, my hands swipe at my blonde strands, shoving it all back behind my ears. Tossing the length over my shoulders, I hunch forward, peering through the shrubs for a while longer.

When the rain gets harder, doe and fawn taking off in the opposite direction. I stand, brushing my hands down my drenched clothes. Smudging the muddied bottom higher on my flared skirt. Sighing, I wander towards a small babbling brook. I kneel against the rough shingle, little rocks biting at my flesh. Taking a piece of fabric in each hand, I dip the floaty white cotton into the cold water, rubbing the dirty spots together below the surface. I watch as the clear water grows cloudy, most of the mud misting off into the brook. I lean back on my haunches, tilting my head up towards the cover of trees, rain splattering against my skin. Knowing I should get back inside the house and clean up before anyone sees, I start to push up to my feet. Using my fingers pressed to the ground to help me up, halfway into a crouch, I stop. Frozen to the spot, my eyes caught on something so desperately beautiful I don't dare move.

After a moment, my breath caught in my lungs, I silently stand. My eyes laser focused on the little furry bundle on the opposite side of the brook. I start across it, my feet slipping on the slimy rocks in the bottom, the cold water lapping just above my ankles, I use my spread arms to help me balance. A tiny fawn lays curled, one of its back legs just brushing the edge of the water. It's long neck covered in a beautiful white speckle. I step closer when it doesn't wake. I glance around for its mother.

Seeing and hearing nothing, I move closer, my feet still in the shallows, I crouch down.

My fingers run down its back, it's soft fur like silk. Its eyes closed, back and chest not moving. I swallow hard. Croaks of toads, the pitter-patter of rain against the leaves, the gentle tweet of bird song high in the treetops. I lay my ear to its nose, hearing and feeling nothing. Taking one last look around, I scoop the scrawny baby up into my bare arms. It's light weight, and sticky fur streaked with goo and blood feels strange against my skin. I cradle the fawn, clutching her close to my partly exposed chest as I make my way back through the forest.

As I pass the horses, I find my discarded cardigan slung over the stable door. Rosie gifted it to me, along with some other soft to touch items. Nothing she gave me is rough or scratchy. I adjust the baby in my arms, wrapping the powder-blue material around its cold little body, hoping a little body heat and comfort will help rouse her from her slumber.

"Grace!" Mother snaps, yelling for me from what sounds like the back door.

I cringe, panic rushing through me, I cast a look over my shoulder. Deciding it best to leave the little baby here. I walk into the stables, passing the stalls with occupants, I make my way to the very end, small bales of hay stacked. I lay the baby down, grabbing handfuls of hay, I pull it apart, separating the rough pieces. I toss them into an empty wheelbarrow, making a nest. Hearing Mother bellow for me again, I recollect the fawn, laying her into the wheelbarrow, my cardigan still swaddled around her. I place some hay over the top of her sleeping form and rush toward the house.

My feet pound over the wet stone path, hopping onto each round rock, I bound my way back to the house. I rush up the steps to the back door, my breathing hard, my skin wet. I push my way into the kitchen, the door slamming shut behind me.

Every head turns in my direction. And there are five new faces also staring back at me. Four so similar to their father and brothers that although I don't know who's who, I know they must be the rest of the Blackwell brothers. All dark hair and shadowed eyes, sun kissed skin and tall, lean bodies. Some wider than others, but all very firm in their stature.

One man though, is very different. Stark white hair, shaved short on his head, luminous green eyes that glimmer like the dark moss climbing tree trunks in the forest. He's the largest, so tall he could easily pass as a giant. He's wearing all black, and there are lots of pockets on his baggy trousers. I can't imagine what any of them are for.

I feel my head tilt, eyes wide and unblinking as they rove across the men in the room. Finally landing on Hunter. His jaw set, straight, black hair covering one eye. I know he's looking at me though, I can feel it. My skin tingles as his chocolate, caramel swirled irises roll down my body, no emotion on his blank face. His brow creasing as his gaze locks on my bare feet. I forget anyone else is in the room as I continue watching his face. Waiting for something, as he surveys me like I'm in a glass cabinet on display for viewing.

"Grace! Good God! What have you been doing?!" Mother shrieks, my gaze dropping to my feet.

My very *muddy* feet. Mother continues to squeal and shriek, pitch getting so high it starts to hurt my ears, but I don't listen to her words. I don't want to be called strange in front of anyone else. I clasp my hands in front of me, knotting my fingers together, which is when I see it.

Blood.

Stryder clears his throat from his place at the table, a couple of the men shift on their feet, one moving to sit at the table too.

"Eleanor, could you give us the room?" his voice echoes around the crowded space.

Mother instantly quiets. I can feel her glare singeing my skin like a forest fire, but all I can hear is the rushing of blood in my ears as the sound of her heels clacking disappears down the hall. My heart pounding inside my chest, my ribs locking it up like a tomb. The creature that's still stuck inside there, claws at my insides and I force myself to swallow past the feeling.

"Grace?" Stryder calls, his deep voice one I'm accustomed to now.

I nod my head, letting him know I'm listening. I have spoken to him a few times in the time I've been staying here. He's a nice man, warm, I'm lucky I have him as my stepfather. I didn't ever have a father that I can remember. Mother said he ran off because of me, because of how I am. That I was too *strange* for him to want to keep me. My chest prickles, my fist automatically coming up to rub the bony valley between my breasts.

"Grace, are you hurt?" Stryder asks me gently and I shake my head, wishing everyone else would just leave, eight sets of eyes focused on me is making my skin hot. "You have blood on your dress," he informs me and I drop my hand from my chest, twisting my fingers together again. Everyone in the room quiet when he says, "it's okay if it's not yours." My gaze snaps up, my neck cracking with the fast motion, eyes focusing in on his. "You won't be in trouble, I promise," he offers, the words sounding sincere.

He speaks to me differently, in a manner unlike the one he uses when he converses with Mother. He's quieter, like I'll be frightened if he talks to me in his usual dark tone.

He thinks I scare easy.

I stretch my spine, standing a little straighter, a little taller. Licking my lips, my hair draped around my face. I inhale, exhale. All of my words are getting jumbled inside of my head, tongue tangling with my teeth. I can't make any words come out. My heart beats so hard I can see my white dress fluttering against my breasts, my chest heaving with rapid breaths.

I don't know what the rules are.

A dark shadow falls across me, encasing me in darkness, a rough finger beneath my chin. I can smell him, his touch lighting me on fire, making me want to squirm, but I refrain somehow. Suddenly a little irritated that he's been gone, and he didn't tell me goodbye. And he left me that night in the dark. And I didn't know when he'd be back. And he called my eyes beautiful instead of strange and I-

"Grace, show me those pretty eyes," Hunter murmurs, tearing me out of my head and slamming me back into the room.

His knuckle still beneath my chin, he raises my head, trying to make me look at him and as much as I desperately want to. Having missed being consumed by his chocolate eyes, I'm mad. I'm dizzy, his scent threatening to overwhelm my every thought. I clench my hands together so tight my knuckles pop. I keep my gaze down, his strong forearm, thick green-blue veins shifting beneath his tanned skin, blocking my vision. I close my eyes, trying not to breathe as he floods my space with him. A tug on a strand of my hair, it's sharp and hard and it makes me gasp with the sting. My eyes automatically pop open, colliding with his and I just stop breathing.

He has stubble shadowing his jaw, a dark bruise through his eyebrow, the one with the jagged, white scar. His top lip is cut and swollen on one side and I zero in on it. Wanting to tear it open, sink my teeth into it and spit the blood back at him. I reach up, unconsciously extending my hand towards his face. He switches out his knuckle for his finger and thumb, pinching my chin hard, he jerks my head up further so I have to arch my neck. The muscles in my shoulders pinching as they stretch into his hold. My eyes locked on his lip; I press the pad of my index finger to the cut. My gaze flicking up to meet his, his eyes smouldering with heat, I claw the wound. My nail tears through the cut, he hisses between his teeth, tightening his grip on me.

"You were gone," I say quietly.

"You mad at me, little sister?" he breathes the words, narrowing his eyes, even as blood drips onto his bottom lip.

He doesn't wipe it away; he lets it trickle down his chin and drip onto his muscular forearm. Hunter isn't a large man, tall, yes, wide, no. He's lean and strong and his entire body is cut and firm with muscles in places I couldn't even name. But I haven't hurt him.

And I want to.

I don't answer. My eyes still on his, they crease at the outer corners as he licks his lips. His tongue moving over each one slowly, the top, then the bottom. He rolls them together, staining them with crimson, stepping back, his hand drops from my face.

"What is the blood from, Grace?" Hunter asks me, his deep tone vibrating through his chest like a rumble of thunder.

I try to step past him, but he blocks me in. His arms either side of me, his fingers curled into the edge of the countertop, caging me in. Bending forward slightly, his face too near, his body too far. But everything all just a bit too much either way. He sucks in a lungful of me, his nostrils flaring, his chest expanding.

"Remember what I said, little sister?" he says against

my lips, his words soaking into me. "Blackwells don't tell lies," he whispers and I tremble.

Hunter tears himself away, spinning as he pulls away from me. Smashing his shoulder into the smirking, white-haired giant, stomping from the room. My eyes trail him until I'm just staring through the open archway into the empty hall.

The white-haired man chuckles, tossing a handful of something from his pocket into his mouth. Crunching loudly, he smiles, showing off all of his white teeth.

"Seems it's not only my family with the weird relationships," he snorts, licking his pink lips.

His eyes drop to my feet, bright emeralds hidden behind thick pale lashes. He drags his gaze up my body, and I feel my cheeks heat uncomfortably. I keep my eyes on him though, I'm surrounded by predators in this kitchen, but this one, this one screams danger.

"Definitely wanna keep this one in the family, Stry," he chuckles again, a deep raspy undercurrent. "I think she's definitely got summink."

I don't understand what it is that he thinks I have, but whatever it is, I don't think I want it. He nods his head to himself, swiping the pad of his thumb over his bottom lip.

"Mm, it's definitely in there, I can practically feel it," he laughs again, a little louder this time.

And I think of the creature that crawled inside my chest.

Can he actually feel it?

"If one of your lot decide they don't want her, send

her my way," he says, flicking his gaze towards Stryder. "Charlie would fucking love to have this one, I'm betting they're on the same level. Anyway," he says flippantly, his tone turning casual, he shoves his hands into two of his many pockets. "I best be getting off, lads. Boss bitch has been riding my arse about the fuck ups at the docks and well, I'm never one to pass up an opportunity to show off my cricket skills," he winks.

Turning towards the rest of the silent men in the room, he steps up, shakes Stryder's hand and follows in the direction Hunter went.

Why anyone would play cricket at the docks is beyond me. Especially as it's getting dark now. How would they see the holes they have to hit that tiny white ball into and shout '*hole in one*'?

"Well," Stryder says, clearing his throat again, even though I don't think he really needs to. "Ignoring my son's outburst, and Eli's wonderful commentary." He purses his lips before continuing. "Why don't we introduce you to the rest of your stepbrothers, Grace? And then we'll get Rosie to serve up some dinner."

Pressing his splayed hands to the tabletop, he glances back up at me. "Then you and I will have a little chat about…" his eyes drop to the blood on my dress, flicking towards the door Hunter left through, before resettling on me. "*That*."

My new brothers are loud. I noticed that they all talk much more than Hunter. They all eat a lot too. Rosie served up endless amounts of food. I didn't know what most of it was, having eaten the same three meals a day for most of my life. But Arrow kept putting spoonful's of food onto my plate so I would try everything at least once. He's very excitable. I was sat between Wolf and Thorne, the two oldest of my six stepbrothers. Thorne is tall and dark, with lots of black lines on his skin, he told me they're called tattoos. I told him I wanted one, he laughed.

Wolf reminds me of Hunter.

He was the quietest, although speaking more words than I've ever heard Hunter say. He sat shovelling spoonful after spoonful of food into his mouth, his thick arm kept brushing against my thin one when he lifted his utensil.

Wolf is a very large man. He is almost as tall as the white-haired giant, Eli, but much broader. His arms are thick, his chest wide, and his thighs are curved and tight in the legs of his trousers. Eyes that are different, like an animal's, a bright yellow-caramel. I bet they glow in the dark. His black hair is long and choppy, he tucked it behind his ears repeatedly before sighing and putting chin length strands up on top of his head. I watched how he did it so I could try later but he told me I have too much, and it would get knotty. Then he told me quietly that I should ask Hunter to help me because he knows how to make the pretty braids that Rosie twists for me.

I kept my gaze down most of the meal, even though the boys kept telling me to look up. I felt as strange, during the whole affair, as Mother always says I am.

Mother, who was as invisible as Hunter during dinner. I'm already concerned with what her absence might mean for me.

I'm in my bedroom now, my hair plaited by Rosie's soft hands before she tucked me up in bed. I smooth my hands down my white silk shorts, the material so soft against my skin it feels as though I'm not wearing anything at all. Padding my way across the cool wood, my fingers curled around the handle, I exit into the hall.

The Blackwell brothers are all staying here tonight, with most of them leaving tomorrow. Not Archer though, he said he has a job to do here before he leaves for his home in a few days. I asked what they did. Stryder said they mainly work in disposals. I guess that's like a dustman.

I tiptoe down the hall, making my way to the staircase. I rush down it as quietly as possible, then head straight for the kitchen, where I know the key is always in the lock and the bolts slide open easily. The air outside is warm when I make my way through the door. The wind blows, tickling my face with loose strands fallen from my braids. I start towards the stables, my bare feet hopping across the leapfrog style pathway, the smooth stone circles cutting their way between the wildflowers.

The light is on above the door helping me find my way in the dark. When I get to it, I reach over the stable door, unlatching it as quietly as I can, closing it gently behind me. The huge horses huff through their noses as I pass by them, their hooves shifting and scuffing over hay covered floors. I stop before the red wheelbarrow, my fingers lightly brushing the straw out of the way to reveal my little fawn.

She's still sleeping, and I wonder what to do, suddenly unsure of my initial intention when I decided to check on her. My teeth chew on the edge of my fingernail as I bring my hand to my mouth, thinking of what I should do with her. I could leave her here until morning, but I don't want her to get cold, because surely mothers would cuddle up to their babies at nighttime. Making my decision I scoop her up into my arms, her furry body still wrapped in my powder-blue cardigan. I clutch her to my chest, using my fingers to pluck out a few stray pieces of hay and hurry back to my room.

I watch from the shadows as Grace sneaks out of her room. Light as a feather on her feet as she ventures through the house and makes her way towards the stables. I follow in the dark, my feet bare like hers as I, too, wade through the long grass. She hurries her steps in a way she thinks she must, as though she thinks if she gets caught doing whatever it is she's doing, she'll be in trouble. She might, dependant on what it is, but Dad is soft with her in a way I've never witnessed him behave before. So even if she killed a man with a hundred witnesses, he'd likely get her off and then take her out for ice cream.

Kicking my leg up, my back leaning against the outside wood panels of the stable, I fold my arms across my chest and wait outside for her to make her reappearance. I can hear the horses shifting in their stalls, likely irritated that she's disturbed them at two-am, that'll make for an interesting ride in the morning. Lady's grumpy when she doesn't get enough sleep.

I stare up at the sky, my head resting against the wall. Millions of stars glittering overhead, the moon a slim crescent above the house. I think of my past two weeks in the city. How I couldn't sleep because there were no stars, no big bright moon high in the sky casting its brilliant beam through my windows. No crickets chirping or toads croaking. Instead, there were car horns blaring at four-am. People laughing drunkenly in the street, throwing their late-night kebabs and smacking the shit out of each other for no other reason than they drank too much.

I hate the city and everyone in it.

It's why I never usually leave the mill. Why I do the disposals down in the small room beside my bedroom when the excess bodies are brought down. I don't have to talk to anyone, see anyone. I don't have to intimidate, torture or beat them unconscious. It's not that I don't enjoy those things. It's just that those things usually involve talking. And I don't really like people, let alone having to converse with them. Dead ones aren't so bad, when I'm cutting into them they're silent. I enjoy the quiet.

My tongue slides across my bottom lip, then the top. The one with a nasty gash through it. The wound that my beautiful eyed little sister tore her fucking nail through. Rage ripped through her irises like a blue flame of hellfire, making my insides twist with forbidden desire. I was instantly rock hard, wanting nothing more than to take her then and there, despite the room filled with my fucking brothers. All of them spent the last two weeks quizzing me over our new stepsister and I've never been more withdrawn. I got overwhelmingly angry every time she was mentioned. My fists curl, knuckles cracking as I think about it.

"Are you still a virgin, Hunter?" Raine dares to ask, my shoulders instantly stiffening up around my ears, the muscles in my back coiling with tension.

"Why is that any of your fucking business, you nosey little cunt," I hiss, venom frothing through my barred teeth.

"I just wondered," he shrugs casually, like he didn't just blurt out a super invasive, personal question.

The fucking audacity of this kid.

"Did you bump your fucking head or something?" I ask bewildered, never has our baby brother ever had such fucking confidence.

He reclines back on the sofa he's seated on, his muscular arms spreading wide, draping across the back of it. His scarred chest bare, still speckled with water droplets from his shower. Having to wash away another man's blood from his skin has clearly made him feel invincible. What a delusional notion. We all have violence etched into our very bones in this family. And just because we share blood doesn't mean I won't beat the shit out of him if he pisses me off.

He scratches his head, fingers clawing through his short, wavy, black hair. His dark brown eyes focusing on me across the room as I sharpen my hunting knife from my perched seat on the armchair. He cocks his head at me, his lips twisting to one side as though in thought. *Running his hand over his burn-marked skin. His fingers trace down the scarred side of his face, the side of this throat, down to his chest, his fingers splay over his heart, mindlessly grazing the rough skin.*

"I only asked because I was interested, I wasn't trying to be an arsehole," he shrugs again like it's normal, then he says, "It's nothing to be ashamed of."

My spine stiffens, hardening like cooled mercury, my eyes narrowing in on my leather handled blade. I pass it between my fingers, distracting myself from the red-hot dousing of an emotion I don't want to feel washing over me. Not liking being under the microscope, I snap back.

"Just because you lot fuck everything with a pulse doesn't mean I have to," I spit at him, raising my eyeballs under my drawn brow.

I glare daggers at him, thinking of a hundred and one ways I could gut him with this little blade. He's my brother and I love him, but this is none of his fucking business.

"Fair enough," he shrugs again, his sepia eyes locked on the ceiling. "I just had some questions about it, that was all."

"Questions? About my fucking dick?" I scoff, rage thrumming through my temples, my eyeballs just about ready to explode inside their sockets.

"Well, yeah, don't you ever get the urge to, ya know… stick it in someone?"

"Raine shut your fucking mouth, brother, before I shut it for you," Wolf snaps. *Clapping his hand around the back of Raine's head, his neck snapping forward with the motion.* "Go help Arrow, you fucking prick," *he orders, dropping into the newly departed space.*

I continue sharpening my knife, rebinding the handle in leather, I wrap it around and around, tucking the end underneath.

"So," *Wolf starts, forcing me to look up, my brow pinching.*

"So what?"

I grind my teeth, eyes narrowing in on him. He hunches forward, elbows on his knees, thighs spread, feet planted. He bows his head, his murky yellow eyes flicking up, all of his features quite literally wolf-like.

"Our new sister-"

"Stepsister," *I hiss in retort, cutting him off before he can finish.*

Chills prickle up my spine, all of my brothers' attention for the last thirteen days has been on what our new little sister is like. Constant badgering questions about her, what's she like, what's her hair colour, eye colour, tall, short, fat, thin? Every fucking question wound me tighter and tighter and if I have to hear one more, I think I may snap.

"You *like* her," *Wolf states, emphasising the word* like, *as though it means… something.*

Not a question. He phrases it like he knows. Like he's crawled inside my fucking skull, cracked it open, forced the pieces apart, sinking himself into the centre of my darkest thoughts. Carelessly throwing a hand grenade into the mix just to finally finish me off. It makes me want to wring his thick fucking neck.

"No, I don't," *the lie twists my guts like it's moulding a balloon animal made of guilt.*

I hurt her.

"You do."

"She's our sister."

"No, she isn't, not really, not by blood," *he says.* "She's eighteen," he tells me like *I* didn't fucking know, and *I* feel my jaw crunching as *I* grind my teeth into dust.

"What the fuck does any of that matter? I don't like her, she irritates the fuck out of me with her stupid fucking hair, and her pale skin and her weird fucking stare. She ain't right," I fume, every single word striking me in the chest like a knife to the heart.

"Riiight, okay."

"I mean it!" I snap, squeezing my knife in my curled fist, the leather creaking in my palm. "I don't know why any of you give a fuck anyway, it's not like you have to live with her. Why do you want to know so much about her?"

"We're interested, Hunter, why is that such a bad thing? She's a new member of our family and naturally, we're curious."

I scoff.

"Naturally curious? There ain't nothing natural about a single one of us in this fucking family. You all just wanna know if she's hot enough to fuck," I spit, fire in my belly roaring with jealousy at the thought of any of their fucking eyes on her.

"Uh-huh," Wolf raises a thick eyebrow, disbelief scrawled all over his face.

"Yes, now, if you don't min-"

"Hunter, why won't you just talk to me about this? You like her, and you've never liked anyone before. I know you, I know how you think, I understa-"

"None of you fucking know!" I bellow, flying up out of my chair. "You don't know *anything!* Stop fucking saying that!"

"Alright, alright, okay," he holds up both hands, palms out towards me, his head sitting up on his shoulders now, facing me properly. "Okay, well, why don't you tell me what you do *feel* about her? You've nearly killed one of us every time she's been *brought up. We can all see that there's more to it than you not liking her. You can't lie to us, brother, we're your family. We only ever want to help you, Hunter, you're my little brother and I love you, man. I know you've got some shit going on, I get that. I know you weren't ever interested in 'sowing your seed' when you were younger, but you are allowed to change your mind. And Grace isn't your sister," he placates, my heaving chest starting to deflate as I exhale slower with every word.*

"I don't want to talk about it, and I don't want to talk about her."

"Okay, if that's what you want," he says standing, his huge frame almost dwarfing mine. He turns towards the door, stopping with his fingers on the handle. "Just know, Hunter, none of us want to be anything to her but her brothers, but that doesn't have to be the same for you," and with that, he leaves, shutting the door behind him.

I sink into the leather armchair, my bare feet pressing into the cold marble floor. I drop my head back, fingers pinching the bridge of my nose. I sigh, willing my traitorous dick to go down as I think of all the things I do fucking like about her.

The stable door unlatches drawing my attention, clicking shut just a moment later as Grace hurries straight past me. Not noticing me at all, she rushes back into the house. Slowly, I make my way up to her room. Climbing the other set of stairs silently, I'm almost at the top when I hear a floorboard creak, the one outside her bedroom that dips if you step too far to the left. I back myself back down the stairs, hearing her approach the staircase I'm on. I wasn't even aware she knew this was here, it's why I've been using it. She's obviously been exploring while I've been away.

What is this girl doing?

She passes me again, standing hidden in the cloak of darkness beneath the curve of the staircase. Deciding to follow at a distance, wanting to see what it is she's up to now, she suddenly freezes before I can make my move to follow. She stands before the dining room, the double doors thrown open, when a sound draws my attention there too. Realising what it is she's seeing, I tilt my head, watching her watch *them*. She's right out in the open, unashamedly watching my brother Archer fuck whichever girl it is he dragged home from the village pub tonight.

Enraptured, she tilts her head, her pale skin and white pyjamas practically glowing in the darkness. Her skinny body hovering like some sort of voyeur ghost.

A low moan drops from the woman's throat, making Grace step forward. Another moan, another step. Her feet almost at the threshold, heat sears through my veins at the thought of her looking at my likely naked brother. Imagining her seeing his dick before mine has me striding down the hall in a red cloud of rage. Despite my bold movements, she doesn't even notice me approaching.

Stepping up behind her, my hand finds its way to her face, slapping over her mouth, lips slightly parted in surprise against my palm. I haul her back against my bare chest, muffling her gasp of surprise, my other arm banding tightly around her waist. I back us up into the shadows, our hiding spot partially covered by a white bust statue. Her hot breath puffs against my hand, my gaze over the top of her head, seeing I was right. Archer has a redhead bent over the dining table, his back to us, his fist in her hair. His bare arse cheeks flexing as he thrusts violently in and out of her.

I grind my teeth, my molars creaking with the motion. Leaning my head forward, my lips brushing over the shell of her ear, I breathe in the scent that I've missed so much over the last couple of weeks.

"You like spying on your brother, little sister?" I hiss at her, my teeth catching her lobe with each word.

She trembles in my hold, her body fully melting into mine, making my entire soul hum with satisfaction. She fits against me so perfectly, I almost hate it. I squeeze her against me, my cock rigid against her small pert arse, nestling itself between her cheeks. She wriggles against me, my chin atop her shoulder, I inhale another lungful of her, damp wood, ferns, and sweet, sweet honeysuckle.

"Well, baby girl? I asked you a question," I whisper against her warm cheek, sliding my hand from her mouth down to the hollow of her throat.

She shivers, my breath tickling down her neck, I run my nose up the side of her throat.

She nods.

"Nu-uh, words, little sister, use that pretty voice for me. Whisper your confession into the dark," I breathe out the instruction, my teeth biting into my bottom lip as she presses her body further back into mine.

"Yes," she whispers, swallowing, her throat bobbing beneath my palm.

I hum against the delicate column of her pale throat, a smirk curving my lips. I squeeze her neck gently, massaging it with thick fingers. Glancing up, my eyes glancing over my brother and his conquest, before flicking back to Grace. Her oddly coloured eyes still locked on the erotic display before her, lips slightly parted as my fingers softly squeeze and release her throat. She licks her lips as Archer pulls out, flips his woman over and slams back into her, grunting as his hips smash into her curved arse. Seeing someone fuck does absolutely nothing for me, but watching Grace watch them turns my already hard cock into granite.

I press my hips into her, pulling her harder against my firm body. Her soft arse cheeks moulding perfectly around the hard length in my joggers. She gasps almost silently, my chest filling with satisfaction as she lets herself fall deeper into me. Sliding my arm down her lithe little body, my fingers gliding over her tummy, a matching white button up shirt covering her. I let my fingers dance over the waistband of her silk shorts.

"Do you know what it is they're doing, little sister?" I question, genuinely curious as to the answer.

It's not that I think Grace is stupid, she isn't. I know that and we've barely had any interaction at all. It's just that, according to Dad, she was never actually *taught* at that fucking *school*. How anyone could palm off that mental institution for a school is fucking beyond me. When he popped up to see us in the city, my brothers bombarded him with questions, and it turns out there's a lot of things Grace doesn't know how to do. It made me angry *at her*.

"No," she whispers nervously, so fucking innocent despite her eyes still locked on the live action porno happening in front of us.

"No?" I repeat her answer back to her, she shakes her head once. "They're fucking, baby girl," I whisper in her ear. "He's sliding his hard dick in and out of her wet cunt because it feels good for both of them," I breathe, my breath fanning loose golden strands across her face. "Does it turn you on?" I purr, the very tip of my index finger slipping just beneath her waistband. "Watching my brother fuck her? Can you feel your pussy getting wet, wanting to feel what she's feeling, to know what it's like?" She tries to turn her head towards me, my grip on her throat tightening. "Nu-uh, keep your eyes on them," I instruct, her entire body trembling in my hold. "Tell me, Gracie, does watching them fuck turn you on?" she squirms in my hold, my thumb firm on the curve of her jaw. "What does it do to you?" I press my chin to the crook of her neck, arching my body over hers, my eyes momentarily flicking to my brother. "If I slide my fingers lower, little sister, will I find your tight little cunt wet for them, or wet for *me*?" I smile then, wide and toothy into the darkness as her body vibrates against mine.

"For you," she hushes in a breathy whisper.

I groan against her soft skin, satisfaction purring through me.

"Hunter, I-"

"*Mmm*, say my name like that again, baby girl," I demand softly, my teeth nipping her throat as she rocks back against me.

"*Hunter*," she gasps, my finger sliding lower beneath her shorts as she drops her head back against my chest.

Her thighs tremble as I slip my hand inside her tiny shorts, the heat from her cunt calling to me like the hot summer sun after surviving a long, frozen winter.

"No knickers again, Gracie," I tut, my middle finger gliding over soft curls to reach her aching centre. I turn my face into her throat, walking us backwards until I hit the wall. "Tell me you want me, baby girl, tell me how much you want your big brother to touch you."

"Hunter?" she groans, her eyes still locked on the scene across the hall.

"Gracie?" I breathe against her warm skin.

"Nobody's ever…" she swallows, licking her lips, her gorgeous eyes finally falling on me as I allow her to roll her head.

"Ever *what*?"

"*Touched* me before," she whispers and it's like a bolt of lightning spears through me.

I squeeze her delicate neck in my hands, feeling the fragile bones flex. The breath rushing out of her as my finger slides down her wet slit.

"You're so fucking wet, Grace," I groan, a rumble tearing through my chest.

Throwing my head back against the wall, I draw her into my body. My palm cupping her cunt, her heat singing me as raw fire floods to her core. I glide my fingertip up and down her slit, my featherlight touch teasing her wet flesh. She drops back against me fully, allowing me to hold her up, trusting me not to let her fall.

A fawn finally snapped between my jaws.

I sigh, my hand cupping her pussy, the other flush with her throat. I drop my nose to her hair, sucking in everything about her, until she's all I can feel thrumming through my veins. My finger slips between her folds, hooking its way through her desire. I tap my sodden fingertip against her swollen clit and the most fascinating noise drops from her throat. I do it again, and again, the same low groan escaping her lips, I watch her face, blissfully entranced by her every little movement. I glide my fingertip through her folds, dragging her arousal up to her clit, tapping it gently before repeating my actions.

My dick grinds between her cheeks, the flimsy material of my worn joggers and the almost transparent silk of her shorts makes it impossible to concentrate on anything else. I forget all about my brother fucking a woman across the hall as Grace's entire body shakes against me. Her thighs clenching, she traps my hand between her legs as she starts to let go.

"That's it, little sister, grind your clit against me, come for your big brother."

Her lips part, her throat arched, I squeeze the breath from her lungs as she grinds her swollen clit into my finger. The rough pad of it rubbing fast, tight circles over her, she explodes. Detonating against me, her entire body trembling against mine, a soft sob escaping her throat. I loosen my grip, she heaves in a lungful of air, her body going fully lax. I thrust my hips against her one last time, my dick pulsing, I come so hard I can hardly fucking see straight.

Both of us gasping for breath, our pants astronomically loud in the silent hall. The hand around her throat drops to band around her waist. Holding her exhausted little body flush against mine, unwilling to let her get even an inch away from me. The wetness in my jogging bottoms seeps through the fabric, soaking into hers. She brings her hand up, her delicately soft fingers skating over my forearm, goosebumps erupting like tiny volcanos all over my olive skin. Her other reaches up, elbow bending, she raises her arm up and over my head. Nails lightly scratching over my scalp, her skinny fingers raking through my thick black hair, she sighs, almost silently. Her warm breath tingles over my bare skin as she relaxes against me, my eyes falling closed, I let my lips find their way to the side of her throat. Pressing against her perfect skin for no more than a second, before they lift to her ear.

"And that, baby girl, *that* is what I'm going to do to you next," I inform her, my deep voice vibrating through her bones, making her shiver.

Straightening, I lift her up into my arms and carry her back to her bedroom.

CHAPTER 9
GRACE

I've never seen anyone fucking before. It's dark and it was a little hard to make out what exactly was going on, but I watched my new brother doing it. And I don't know how I feel about it. It made me curious, to want to see what was happening. But I don't think it really affected me.

Not until Hunter.

Pouncing out of the shadows, striking me like I was his prey. When he grabbed me, held me and whispered to me. When he touched me, and made my body do something new. *Come.*

I like the way he makes me feel when he presses his rough fingers into my flesh. He left me dotted with tiny little bruises last time, I kept poking them to make them last longer while he was away. Every time I saw or felt them it made me feel better, even when they hurt. I liked it.

He makes me feel… *seen.*

I close my eyes as Hunter carries me through the darkness, his huge hands on my much smaller body make me feel safe. My head lying against his strong chest, his warm skin against my cheek, his steady heart-beat drumming in my ear. I snuggle into him, never having had anyone clutch me so close before. Nobody's ever wanted to be close to me before in case they expose themselves to my disease and catch what I have.

But not Hunter, he doesn't seem to care about that. Not when he keeps finding ways to touch me, or breathe me in. He held my hand in the forest that first day, without hesitation, he cupped my face and played with my hair. Hunter breathes me in like I'm his air and he can't survive even one second without sucking in a lungful of me when we're near each other. Even when I'm dirty and my clothes are messy, and I have mud between my toes and leaves in my hair.

Hunter holds me like I mean something. Like he cares if he drops me, something he values, doesn't want to let go of. His thick, strong fingers pinch into my skin, and I sigh as he holds me closer as we start to ascend the stairs.

Opening my eyes, I look up at him through my lashes, staring at his ruggedly masculine features. His straight nose, full lips and sharp jaw. His dark eyes like twinkling galaxies in the pitch dark. The jagged white scar glinting through his eyebrow, his new bruise and split lip. I almost smile looking at his pretty mouth.

I made him bleed.

When we make it to the top of the back staircase, he

effortlessly takes us through the upper floor. Turning along corridors, bypassing the rooms the rest of his brothers are currently sleeping in. As we make it to my bedroom door, he adjusts me slightly in his grip, freeing his hand to depress the handle. I was so lost inside my own head I almost forgot about the thing I have hiding up here.

In a panic, I squirm in his hold, his grip tightening on me, but with one hand still on the door handle I manage to drop my legs down, the rest of my body spilling out of his arms. I twist to face him. My back to the door, his chest almost touching mine, his hand still firmly on the handle. I look up at him, my chest heaving from my struggle. He plants his free hand on the wall beside my head, dipping his own so he's face to face with me.

"Whatever you're hiding, little sister, I'm going to find it. So why don't you just tell me what it is that you've done *before* I find out for myself?" he raises an eyebrow, his nose almost touching mine.

I let out a shaky breath, my eyes locked on my fingers pressing against his solid chest. I swallow, wondering what he'll think. I didn't steal her from her mother, she left her there, abandoned her, I'm saving her. I went to get milk, but then Archer…

"Grace." Hunter's voice cracks like the whistle of a whip, my eyes snapping up to his.

I breathe hard, my fingertips digging into his hard muscles, my nails gouging little crescent shaped marks into his smooth, tanned skin. He watches me, unflinching even as I draw blood. His dark eyes running all over my face, my teeth dig into my lip, tongue sticking to the roof of my mouth.

"Tell me what I'm going to find, little monster," he whispers against my lips, making me tremble.

I wish I were braver. I wish I could lean forward and press my lips to his. But I don't. And I can't. That's what people who love each other do. Hunter doesn't love me; he just likes to hurt me and I him.

"Why, little monster?" I manage to choke out, my eyes dropping to my slick fingertips.

Even in the dark I know he's bleeding, that *I* made the tiny wounds his life force drips from. I hook my nails into his flesh, digging and curling them in as hard as I can. Hunter's breathing picks up, his chest heaving, the tip of his nose pressing against my own. His breath against my parted lips. I wish I could see him better, know what he's thinking, watch those deep, dark eyes swirl like little vortexes.

We're always in the dark, Hunter and I. Never together in the daylight like normal people are. Maybe Hunter isn't normal either. Perhaps he's more like me.

"Because," he breathes against my lips, his plump pout grazing over my mouth. "It takes one to know one," he whispers, his words wrapping around my own tongue as I consume his warm breath in my mouth. "And I, little sister, scented the monster in you the very first moment I laid eyes on you in that dark forest." He licks his lips, his tongue catching my bottom one. "You could never hide what you are from me."

I heave in a breath as Hunter pushes his hips against mine, forcing me back against the cool wood of the door. The back of my bare arms prickling with goose-bumps at the sudden drop in temperature against my heated skin. His dick prods into my lower belly, hard and thick and so, so hot, I can feel it radiating through his thin jogging bottoms. He nuzzles his face into the crook of my neck, groaning as he does, sucking in my scent. My nails carve deeper into his chest, when suddenly I'm falling backwards.

Hunter thrusts the door open behind me, his free arm dragging me into his chest as my feet scramble to make purchase. He charges us through the open door-way, my breath rushing from my lungs as he closes the door almost silently, spins and thrusts me against it. My head thuds against the solid wood, stars shooting across my vision, as he crowds me in. His thick arms like steel bars trapping me between them. He rolls his hips against mine, forcing me to remember the dampness inside my silk shorts.

"Now," Hunter starts, venom on his tongue.

Moonlight falling in through my large window reveals the sadistic glint in his rich, ebony eyes. I swallow hard as my heart tries to climb its way up my throat, a knot in my stomach. I blink at him, his eyes flicking between mine. He lifts a hand from the door beside my head. His fingers slowly smoothing their way down my braid, he sweeps his hand to the bottom of the plait, twisting the tied-off end between his thumb and finger.

"What have you got hidden up here, Gracie?"

Hunter's rasp ripples down my spine, making me arch away from the wall, an invisible string pulling me towards him. He tugs on my hair, drawing my eye, I watch as he cords the long golden rope around his fist, all the way up until his knuckles graze my chin. I whimper as he pulls hard, my scalp screaming, my blood hot.

"Show me what you have tucked away up here, little monster, show me all your secrets," he hisses into the dark.

I look up into his eyes, determined not to show him anything. I'm already upset with him for leaving me. This isn't even any of his business.

"No."

"No?"

"No."

He chuckles, the sound cold and threatening. Just as he turns away from me, facing into the room, he takes a step toward the centre of the space and wrenches my head with him. I try to pull back, his fingers knotted in my hair, I'll do whatever it takes to keep him away from her.

"Gracie," he says in wonder. "Why is there a lump in your bed?"

I pull away sharply, feeling thick strands of hair snap inside his fist, but it's no use, he doesn't loosen his hold, doesn't let me go. And I hate that I don't really want him to. Anything to keep him touching me. Being in my space. I never want Hunter to leave me again.

"There isn't," I retort, making him turn his head sharply over his shoulder.

He peers at me, brow dipped low over his narrowed eyes.

"What did I say about lying?" he quizzes, pausing very obviously for an answer.

"Blackwells don't tell lies," I whisper the phrase that secretly makes my heart warm, it means I belong somewhere.

"Good girl," he coos, half of his face bathed in light from the moon. "Now," he starts, walking me over to my bed. "You're going to continue being a good girl and lift the blankets for me to see," he finishes, stopping us at the side of the bed, our bodies directly angled towards the huge window.

"Promise you won't get mad at me," I request.

I glance down at the sheets, then back up at Hunter, his eyebrow raised, eyes locked on me. I chew on my lip, my fingers shaky, the tips flecked with *his* dried blood.

"You won't be in trouble," he reassures me.

A statement.

I bend forward, my fingers curling over the hem of the quilt, white with little blue flowers, and pull it back. Hunter doesn't move, I don't move. I just stare down at my beautiful little fawn, her red-brown fur and white speckled back. The moon bathing her in angelic light.

"What did you do to it, Gracie?"

"*Do*?" I question, my nose crinkling, I look up into Hunter's stern face. "I didn't *do* anything to her, she's sleeping."

"Grace," Hunter's deep voice is louder now, his fingers squeezing the hair in his fist.

He licks his lips, his eyes on my baby, before he finally looks at me, studying my face in the shadows. He turns me towards him, unravelling my long hair, uncurling his tight grip. My scalp tingles, his big, warm hands settling on my slim shoulders, his thumbs dancing across my collarbones through the silky fabric. I tilt my head, gazing up into his handsome face.

"I can be her mother, her other one left her all by herself near the water. It isn't kidnapping, I saw her leave."

"Grace," Hunter says my name and the words on my tongue dry up. "This fawn," he starts, glancing momentarily back at the bed.

His warm hand comes up, cupping my face, his thumb on my cheekbone. He drops his head to mine, forehead to forehead, breathing me in. Drawing back slowly so I can look into his dark brown eyes.

"I have to take her back to her mother, okay?" he says quietly.

"But-"

"What you did was a good thing, you thought you were helping. I know that, baby girl," he looks at the fawn again, my eyes following his. "But I need to take her back now," he whispers.

My bottom lip wobbles as I look at her lying in my bed, her little head resting atop her tiny hoof.

"But her mother left her," I whisper, my watery eyes

blurring my vision, my fingers aching to reach out and touch her.

I press the heel of my hand to the centre of my chest, the creature that somehow crawled its way inside me hurting my heart. Twisting and pinching the heavily thudding organ trapped beneath my ribcage. I feel a sickness in my tummy when I think of a little girl being left somewhere by herself. How her mother abandoned her in a big scary place and how the people there were frightening and cold. How they liked to use their fists and nasty words as punishment when she didn't follow the rules.

Nobody gave me any rules here.

"Her mother just left her there, leaving her to survive all by herself. Abandoning her in an unfamiliar place. No one ever teaching her how to read or how to swim. How she's going to grow up still not knowing how to do any of those things," a sob gets caught in my chest. "I just wanted to save her, Hunter. I don't want her to be lost and lonely!" I wail, big fat tears sluicing down my face, a cry rattling inside my lungs.

Hunter's grip leaves my shaking shoulders. My legs giving out beneath me, but instead of crashing to the floor, Hunter's there. His thick arms banding around my lower back. He drops to the wooden floor on his bum, pulling me between his parted thighs, sweeping me across the floor. Clutching me tightly to his chest, his nose in my hair, his hands wrapped protectively around my trembling body. I sob against his naked skin, my hands curled around his forearms. My tears mixing with the blood I drew, he runs a hand over my head, his palm at my crown. He massages his thick fingers into my scalp, a light pressure drawing my head beneath his chin.

He swivels us around, his back resting against the side of the wooden bed frame. Lifting my legs over his thigh, his other leg wrapping around me. Cocooning me in, making me safe.

"It's okay, baby girl," Hunter whispers in the dark, his rough voice, thick and deep, wraps around me the same way his arms do.

And that's how we stay, the two of us together.

Wrapped up in one another in the dark.

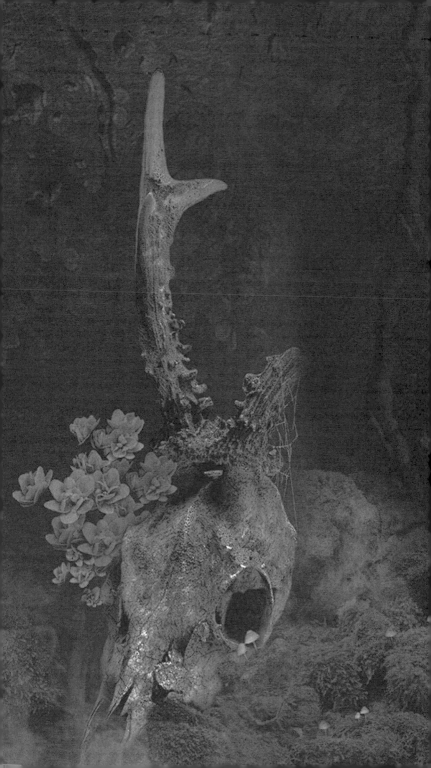

CHAPTER 10
HUNTER

I smooth my hand over her soft hair, her face nuzzled into my bare chest. Her breaths deep and even. My mind ticks over, so many things violently rushing through it. Every thought conflicting with the last. I don't even know where to begin with picking through this mess. I mean, for starters, there's a dead deer in this girl's bed and she's convinced herself it's sleeping. Well, I think that's what she's done. Does she understand the concept of death? I knew she was innocent but I'm not sure I realised just how much. And if her comments on reading and swimming were anything to go by, I'm pretty sure I'm in a *very* complex situation here.

I peer over my shoulder, eyes squinting in the dark, the bed sheets pulled back, moonlight exposing the fragile fawn. It's clear to me, even in the darkness that Grace didn't kill it. She may have some violent tendencies, but she's not a murderer. I look down at her small body in my lap, her translucent skin highlighted by the green and blue veins snaking through her chest. Her heartbeat thumps against my palm settled on her back, her warm breaths ghosting over my chest. Blood and tears dried on my naked skin, a piece of me, a piece of her, entangled together.

I drop my head back against the edge of the mattress, staring unseeingly at the ceiling. I sigh, my hands gently stroking Grace's body, her skin an addiction I just can't quit. Beautiful and unblemished and so. Fucking. Soft. It's all I've thought about for the last two weeks. Like a splinter buried deep beneath the skin, I know it's there, but I just can't seem to get it out. She's overtaken my every waking thought, even occupying my usually dreamless sleep.

Her beautifully unusual eyes, one an ice blue, the other a warm hazel, so wide and innocent and pure. Her soul bathed in white light, an iridescent glow, her aura so comforting and bright. I see it all and I want nothing more than to plunge my darkness inside of her like a thick blade. Draw out those shadows I know she hides away deep inside. Force her to see it's okay, to embrace it. To let it fester and grow instead of hiding it away. Show her that when she hurts me, I thrive, and she thrives too. I sense the sadistic part inside of her, a tiny, splintered fragment of darkness in her chest that I want her to cling on to.

It calls to me.

The need to corrupt her.

I want to own her, mind, body and sick little soul.

Twist and turn the parts of her until there is nothing left but what I put there. A sickness flows through my blood, depravity thick and rife in my veins. The darkness that calls to me like a siren I welcome with open arms. The hole in my heart, the one carved out, could be so easily filled by Grace. It's a gaping, gushing wound but she could be the brutal answer.

I don't know how long I sit for, but the darkness starts to fade and my spine twinges with pain from sitting on the wooden floor. I pull Grace tighter to my chest, lifting her into my arms, I tuck my knees beneath me, before rising onto one foot then the other. I round the bed, tucking her frail body beneath the quilt, I pull the blankets up to her chin. My fingers dusting stray gold hairs off of her face, she sighs. My hand automatically cupping her cheek, she settles into the palm of my hand. Wanting, for the first time in my life, to climb in beside her. I've never wanted to hold someone like I want to hold her. I glance across the mattress, the dead deer likely seeping fluid into the sheets. I slide my hand from Grace's face. Sighing heavily, I move away from the sad girl in the bed and get to work removing the fawn.

The rain beats down violently on my back, poking at my skin like needles, stinging as it hits my flesh. I drive the shovel deeper into the mud, the hole I'm digging continuously filling with rainwater. I slam the metal deeper and deeper, my feet sinking into the marshy ground. Thunder rumbles in the distance, thick clouds lying low in the early morning sky. Blocking out the light, swamping the land in darkness. Once I'm down as deep as I'm going to get in this weather, I lay the cardigan wrapped fawn in the bottom, sweeping the thick sludge into the hole. Watching the fragile animal disappear as I cover it over.

I throw the shovel down outside the stables as I pass, trudging my way up the stone path. When I make it down to my bedroom, I slump back against the door as it closes behind me. Tyson and Duke pop their heads up, their big, lean bodies curled into one another atop my bed. I sigh heavily, stripping off my sodden clothes, leaving them where they land as I head into my ensuite. Stepping inside the two-person shower, a deep jade stone with chrome fixtures, I flick the water on. My hands splayed against the wall, head dipped between my shoulder blades as freezing water sputters from the waterfall shower head before it warms up, my muscles simultaneously screaming. I don't know how long I stand like that, but it's long enough for me to be scalded by the spray and then plunged back into ice. Reluctantly I dry off, running a towel over my hair, throwing it into the tub, brushing my teeth before dressing in joggers and a tight t-shirt. I pull my boots on, whistle for both dogs to follow and head up to the stables to start the day.

A while later, I let myself in the back door to the staff kitchen, why it's called that I don't know, because it's where we all seem to accumulate at all hours of the day. The rain cleared up, allowing me to release the horses out into their paddock for a while. Grazing the meadow while the sun's shining will make a change, this has been the wettest September in years, despite it being so unseasonably warm.

I stop in my tracks as I enter. Grace is sat at the table, a pile of pills laid out before her on the yellow polka dot tablecloth. Her eyebrows knitted together, head bowed, lips pulled into her mouth, she sits on her hands. Eleanor bent over her as she leans across the table. Her neck twisted over her shoulder, wicked gaze on me as I stare at her.

"What's going on in here?" I ask roughly, my blood already running hot at whatever situation I've walked in on.

Grace doesn't look up at me, she doesn't even flinch at the sound of my voice, making me frown harder. I turn to the sink, my back to them. Pushing up my long sleeves, I switch on the taps with my elbows, sticking my hands beneath and soaping them up. I start to wash, willing my temper not to flare, my eyes unblinking as I methodically foam and lather soap up to my elbows.

"Why did you not take these last night?" Eleanor hisses, "you know you are to take your pills every night or you don't get to stay here. That was the condition."

I hear her nails drum against the thick plastic table-cloth, and I sink my teeth into my lip so hard I hear the skin pop with pressure. I breathe in through my nostrils.

"Answer me, Grace!" she finally snaps after a few long seconds of silence.

"I didn't…" Grace trails off.

"You didn't what?" Eleanor retorts sharply.

"I don't know the rules," Grace says quietly.

Eleanor scoffs loudly, "take them," she demands, sniffing when she says, "now."

"But they'll make me go to sleep," Grace whispers brokenly, making me grit my teeth, my hands squeezing the edges of the sink as I lean over it, the water still running.

"Well, you should have thought about that last night when you didn't swallow them down then, shouldn't you," Eleanor spits spitefully and I have to squeeze my eyes shut to stop myself from snapping Eleanor's fucking neck. "Take them right now, Grace, we're not leaving this kitchen until you've swallowed every single last one. Now, swallow. Don't look at me!"

"Can I please have some water?" Grace requests, voice shaking on an exhale.

"No. Little girls that don't follow rules, don't get rewards. Now swallow."

I hear the slightest movement, Eleanor huffing, I exhale sharply through my nose.

"Hurry up!" Eleanor snarls.

Grace swallows loudly, gagging a little as she does and I fucking snap.

Spinning around to face them, I rush Eleanor, a chair flying across the floor as I barrel past it. My hand clamps around her scrawny throat, her head smacking into the wall beside the archway as I slam her into it. Crowding her in, my fingers flexing on her throat. She squirms in my hold, her eyes wide with fear as I angle my free forearm across her chest, water from my skin soaking us both. I feel the smirk curl my lips, rolling up over my teeth in a snarl, I get in her face until we're nose to nose. My dark eyes flicking between her dead hazel ones. So much like my Gracie's, yet so not.

How does this woman think she can treat someone that way? Her own fucking daughter.

"I am fucking *sick* of so-called *mothers* treating their children like shit," I spit, my fingers flexing against her fragile windpipe. "What makes you think you can come into my fucking house and treat *anyone* that fucking way? Especially your own fucking daughter, you disgusting bitch," I breathe heavily, my chest hitting hers with every uneven inhale.

Large hands grab at my arms, my brother's voice echoing around my skull as I shrug him off. Eleanor's wide eyes growing redder, blood vessels bursting in her beady little eyeballs, doing nothing but encouraging my strength. Her nails continue clawing at my forearm, drawing blood, and gouging at my flesh. Shouting in the background, stronger hands on my arms. Blood rushes through my veins like bubbling lava, buzzing in my ears, a roaring fire in my belly. I squeeze tighter, Eleanor's face turning an ashy shade of blue when I'm pulled back, her body slumping to the floor. Strong arms bind around me, pulling me back against a wide chest. Wolf's amber scent filling my nostrils, making me stiffen.

Thorne stares between me and Eleanor, an unhappy expression on his usually stoic face.

"Are you all right, Eleanor?" Thorne asks, making me snap my teeth at him.

He shoots me a sharp look, telling me not so subtly to shut the fuck up and calm down. Wolf tugs me a step back, his arms locked through mine, his huge body hauling me back another step. My chest heaves, my mouth foaming as rage burns through me. My vision clouded in red. Eleanor claws at her throat, coughing and spluttering and I pray she bites off her own tongue and chokes on it, or at least drowns in the blood. She finally straightens up, still hacking a cough and glares at me. I lunge for her again, held back by Wolf keeping a tight hold on me.

"Pack it in!" Thorne's deep voice cracks like a whip, my lungs deflating slightly at the order. "Now, I don't know what's going on in here, but enough is enough!" Thorne commands, making the entire kitchen fall silent.

Nothing but my heavy breathing and Eleanor's husky spluttering can be heard until the fucking bitch sucks in a breath and turns her glare back on me. My spine strengthens to steel, and I feel myself physically grow as my temper soars to new heights. Wolf's grip tightening on my arms, she raises her hand, her finger pointing in my face, and it takes everything in me not to bite it the fuck off.

"Just wait until your daddy hears about this, boy," she threatens, and I lunge.

Thorne steps between us, blocking her from me. He

presses into my front, Wolf flush to my back, crowding me between them, my arms still twisted with his.

"Stop, brother, she's not worth it," Thorne tells me, his voice low, breath against my lips.

His ebony eyes boring into my own, I nod, dropping my gaze, he steps away.

"I'll have you packing your bags by the end of the week, you stupid boy," Eleanor rasps cockily like she didn't just have my hands around her throat.

I pull against Wolf's hold, despite knowing I'd never escape him.

"Don't threaten me you fucking cunt, and don't you dare speak to Grace like that in front of me ever again. If I catch you, I'll slit your fucking throat. You think you're something so fucking special, boning my *daddy* for designer fucking shoes," I scoff, rolling my eyes. "You think you *mean* anything to him? You're just something to pass the time, *sweetheart*," I spit, my eyes dragging down her body, lip curling into a snarl. "I don't see anything special," I cock a brow, giving her the most unimpressed expression I can muster, making *her* lunge for *me*.

I chuckle darkly as Thorne hauls her back. Her, what would be classed as pretty, face contorts in anger, colour returning to her cheeks in the form of a violent blush.

"You little shit!" she shouts, making me laugh louder.

"Look," I say, blowing out a breath, rolling my eyes like I couldn't give a single fuck. "It's not that you're an unattractive woman, it's what's inside of you that spoils your pretty fucking face. I hate to be the one… no, wait, I *love* to be the one to inform you of this. You can't cure rot." I shrug. "That's just how it is. It's going to eat you alive from the inside out, destroying everything its possessed, you desperate fucking whore."

I watch as she shouts at me, hearing nothing as I tune her screechy voice out. Spittle flying from her mouth as she presses forward, despite Thorne holding her back, before removing her completely as she bellows down the hall. I don't hear a single fucking word of her poison. My smug smirk morphing into a snarl as I think about hacking her up into little pieces. Snarl twisting into a sharp, deadly smile at the thought when I suddenly feel *her*.

My head snaps over my shoulder, nearly colliding with Wolf's face in the process, his grip loosening on me as he feels my body deflate completely. My tongue goes heavy in my mouth as I turn fully towards her. Her feet pulled up on the chair, knees to her chest, hands smashed down over her ears as she rocks back and forth. Her eyes squeezed shut as my younger brother Arrow holds her. His dark eyes pinched with concern as he watches her. His large hand smoothing over her hair. It's down today, heavy, thick curtains of spun gold spilling down and around her shoulders.

'She doesn't know how to do her own hair, teach her how to braid it, Hunter.'

Wolf's voice echoes in my mind, the memory of him unknowingly encouraging my obsession.

I step around the table, Raine and Archer both stepping away from where they were crowded around her back, a protective wall. I crouch down beside her, my fingers finding her beautiful face. Her small nose, the tip slightly upturned, a single freckle beneath her left eye I know to be hazel beneath her closed lid. I trace her lips with my thumb, my other hand reaching up, closing around her slim wrist, I gently draw her arm down, pulling her hand away from her ear. I smooth my thumb in soothing circles over the back of her hand, my thumb on her lip dropping to her chin.

"Gracie," I whisper, her eyes fluttering slightly. "Look at me, baby girl," I coax, not giving a single fuck that my brothers are all here listening. "I'm sorry," I tell her softly, my deep voice vibrating up my throat. "I didn't mean to scare you," I promise as her eyes draw up to mine. "There she is," I hush, my hand moving to cup her face as she looks down at me. "I'm sorry."

She looks at me, an adorable confusion on her face, she blinks hard.

"You didn't scare me," she whispers back.

I glance up at Arrow who shrugs his shoulders, mouth pulled down into a frown. My gaze flicks to his caressing fingers, he immediately removes his hand from her hair to rest on the back of her chair instead and I feel my shoulders relax.

"I didn't?" I question, looking back at Grace, my head cocked.

She shakes her head, pulling her bottom lip between

her teeth, eyes on her hands. Her lip pops free, her tongue smoothing over the reddened skin.

"I didn't want her to hurt you," she whispers vulnerably, and I feel that organ lying dormant inside my aching chest flutter to life, the way it does every time I'm close to her.

A small smirk cracks across my lips at the thought of her tiny mother hurting me.

"Grace, look at me," hesitantly her gaze lifts. "She didn't hurt me," I assure her.

Her eyes run over my face as if making sure.

"You're sure?" she breathes out.

I lean in, my hand cupping the back of her head, drawing her face down towards mine. I press our foreheads together, breathing in a deep lungful of her scent. Sweet honeysuckle, earthy ferns. I sigh, letting my eyes fall closed in contentment.

"I'm sure," I whisper against her lips.

"I'm sorry, Hunter" she whispers the words over my mouth.

My fingers tighten in her hair, a chill running down my spine at the sound of my name on her tongue.

"Why?" I ask, drawing back enough to look at her.

"It's my fault," she swallows. "I didn't take my pills," she confesses the sin solemnly.

I shake my head, her small hand coming up to rest against my chest. I instantly settle, the riled beast inside of me cooling down at her gentle touch.

"Grace, what she said, what she did. You know that's not right; she can't treat you that way. You have nothing to be sorry for, baby girl. You did nothing wrong."

"What are these for anyway?" Archer asks loudly, turning the large handful of pills over in his open hand, causing my eyes to narrow in on him.

I'm about to snap back with something sarcastic but Grace speaks before I can.

"I don't know," she whispers, "but they make me feel worse on the inside."

"What do you mean, baby girl, worse than what?"

"Worse than when Mother calls me names or tells me I'm-"

"Tells you you're what?" Raine chimes in and I force myself to exhale slowly.

She looks up at him, craning her neck awkwardly before looking back at me.

"Tells me I'm *strange*," she half chokes out the last word and I want to love and destroy her all in the same moment. "All of my insides get knotted," she continues. "But then it disturbs the creature in here," she explains, running her knuckles up and down her breastbone.

I frown, looking from her exposed chest back up to her face.

"Creature?" Wolf asks now, his heavy mellow tone rumbling around us.

She frowns a little, her pale eyebrows drawing together, she wrinkles her nose. And it takes everything inside of me not to bite the tip of it as it dances on her face.

"Well, sometimes, since I left my school," I grit my

teeth at the word school. "I can feel it in here," she whispers, looking down at her chest.

"What does it feel like?" Raine asks, staring at her with his mouth popped open in wonder.

I want to jump up and slam it shut. Tell him she's not some science experiment for him to gawk at. But I don't, instead, noticing all four of my remaining brothers look at her in fascination. I suppose I'm silently intrigued by her answer too.

"It prickles and pinches at my heart."

"When does that happen, Gracie?" I coax her gently, hearing her soft voice be so confused makes my insides churn.

"When I'm hurting," she whispers, looking at me for... *something.*

I nod, glancing up at my brothers, all of them understanding my silent request without the need of spoken communication. They all shuffle out of the kitchen, leaving us alone.

"That's not a creature, Gracie."

"It's not?" she questions quickly, her head snapping up to stare at me in awe as I straighten to stand.

I shake my head, offering her my hand, she takes it without hesitation. Her delicate fingers sliding into my large palm, I lace them between mine and take us outside.

CHAPTER II
GRACE

I stare down at Hunter's big hand swamping my smaller one as we walk towards the meadow instead of the forest. He didn't make me put any shoes on when we passed them by at the back door. He glanced down at my bare toes, and I swear I saw him smile as he pulled me out the door. I like feeling the dirt beneath my feet.

The sun is high in the sky, no clouds in sight as far as I can see. I squint up, my lashes helping block out the light, as I let the sun's warmth wash over my face. My hair hanging loosely down my back, my white sundress blowing around my thighs in the gentle breeze. I let Hunter lead me out into the overgrown field. The grass up to my knees, red poppies, tiny blue flowers and white daisies dance around my ankles.

I squeeze Hunter's hand a little tighter as I spot what we seem to be heading towards. My footsteps slow a little, my eyes lock on its huge black body, glistening like diamonds beneath the sun. Hunter keeps walking, my pace dragging behind his just a little. I peer up at him, finding his gaze already on me. An intense look in his dark eyes, he tugs on my hand, pulling me closer, until we're stopping before the huge black horse.

Hunter looks at me as he releases my hand and I instantly miss his touch. He moves toward the beautiful creature, which looks up at him as he approaches. Running his large hand up and down the front of her face, she drops her head forward further, encouraging his touch. I curl my fingers into my palms, sucking my lip between my teeth as I watch her huff into his palm. Nodding her head up and down as he produces a carrot out of his pocket. I laugh as she tries to nab it, but he holds it back, patting her firmly on her neck. Turning to look at me over his shoulder, he flashes me a small smile, and my heart flutters.

"Come here, Gracie," he calls softly, his hand with the carrot outstretched towards me, the other on the horse's nose.

My belly flip-flops, heart soaring as I take a hesitant step forward. I've never been this close to a horse before, I've passed them in the stables, but I've never touched one. I've not really looked at them either. This horse is huge, its long, lean legs have long fluffy hair around the ankles, and hair over its neck almost as long as mine. The horse fusses, presumably impatient for the carrot, scuffing its foot into the tall grass. I pause in my approach, unsure if it wants me closer. Hunter inclines his head towards me, silently summoning me forward and my feet answer him, unconsciously padding me closer.

"This is Lady," Hunter tells me in his usual quiet, but deep tone and the tightly wound muscles in my body start to uncoil.

I stare up at him, my mouth popped open a little. Retaking my hand, he presses the carrot into my palm, curling my fingers over it.

"Tuck your thumb in so she doesn't accidently catch it," he warns me, using his thick fingers to manoeuvre my thumb out of the way. "Here," he pulls my arm upwards, closer to the horse, she snorts into his hand, the one cupped around her nose. "Just like this," he explains, covering my hand with his much larger one, guiding the carrot nearer Lady.

She turns her head toward me, Hunter patting her with his now free hand, still guiding me with the other. Lady's lips roll back revealing, huge, straight, yellowed teeth, she dips her head forward and suckles the carrot from my hand, I let it go as she pulls it gently from between my shaky fingers, small hairs on her lips tickling my palm. A smile pulls at my lips as I look up at Hunter.

He's already watching me.

His hand still locked around mine, rolls down, his fingers securing my wrist. Dark eyes shining like melted chocolate in the light, those warm honey specks glowing under the bright sun like gold. Raising my hand higher, adjusting his grip on my wrist, he slides his fingers further up my arm. Chills racing across my skin despite the warm sun, his eyes forever locked on mine. I want to look away, to drop my gaze to my toes, stare at the tops of my muddy feet. I don't. Instead, I hold his dark stare as his mouth meets my flesh, soft, plump lips pressing hard to the inside of my wrist. So unlike the brutality of the Hunter I know. I couldn't stop the involuntary shiver if I tried. Rolling up my spine like a bolt of electricity, prickling in the nape of my neck. I tremble as his lips part, his teeth grazing my skin, climbing higher, his eyes still firmly on mine. I daren't even blink, think, *breathe*.

He pulls me closer, his lips working their way across my goosebump smattered skin. His lips meet the crook of my elbow, just as my free hand plants itself against his cotton covered chest. Keeping him away but wanting to drag him closer. Tingling starts in the soles of my feet, warmth spreading through my lower belly as his tongue leisurely rolls up the inside of my bicep. I'm arching backwards now, my fingers clutching the black fabric of his t-shirt, twisting my handful of stretchy cotton into a fist. His big body leans over me, one hand still on my wrist, the other sliding to the base of my spine. He fists his big hand in the thin cotton of my white dress, twisting the excess fabric in his fingers, sharply hauling me closer. I gasp, our bodies touching in every possible place they could in this position.

He quickly works his leg between my thighs, dress bunched up high between them, rough against the sensitive skin there. Hunter drops my arm, smoothing his large palm over my shoulder, up the side of my throat, settling in the back of my hair. He turns his face into the crook of my neck, his body engulfing mine, blocking the sun out with his large shadow. I ease against him.

It's where I feel safest.

In the dark.

With *him*.

My eyes close, my lungs drawing in the deepest breath, and it's all him. Hunter is a living breathing embodiment of the forest; moss, daisies, the cool stream that flows through the very centre of the trees. He floods my system with his scent, his teeth catching the delicate skin of my collarbone. I let my head drop back on my shoulders, exposing the thumping beat of my heart in the form of my pulse. Fluttering just beneath the pale skin of my throat. I feel Hunter's grip tighten, his nose running up the side of my neck, his hand tangling itself further in my hair. He stops when his nose is just below my ear, his lips over my quickening pulse, it thuds against his parted pout. My breath tight in my chest, he grinds his muscular leg against my bare pussy, and I groan low in my throat, the fabric of his tight-fitting joggers causing a rough friction.

"I love this perfect fucking skin, little sister," Hunter rasps, his lips, tongue and teeth whispering over my pulse point, nipping and sucking.

Heat roars through my veins, warmth stirring in my belly. My free hand grips his bicep, nails carving into his skin, I pinch my fingers tightly to him, entire body thrumming. His teeth sink into my neck, I squirm, white spots dancing behind my closed eyelids at the burst of pain. I go lax in his hold, until he grinds his thigh harder into my pussy. That has me stiffening, my muscles screaming for him to do it again. His jaws locked around my throat, warm saliva dribbles between his lips, running down my neck as he suckles hard. Pulling and popping as he tugs and releases the skin. He runs his mouth sloppily up my throat, tasting me with his tongue, swirling it over my skin.

Hunter breaks away from me, straightening us up, my body instantly feeling cold at his departure. His nose dropping to touch mine, dark eyes full of fire flicking between my own.

"Open your mouth, baby girl" he instructs quietly.

Fisting my hair, he snaps my head back, bones cracking with the sharp motion. I swallow, opening my mouth, pain tingling in the top of my spine.

"Wider," he grunts, his hand from my back going to my jaw, squeezing hard, forcing me to open my mouth as wide as I can. His tight grip makes my teeth ache, "stick out your tongue."

I do as he says without conscious thought, his eyes on mine, he spits on my tongue. I blink, confused, go to close my mouth.

"No," he snaps, "keep your tongue out," his grip on my jaw tightens.

A blush creeps up my chest, heating my cheeks, as Hunter's eyes focus on his spit in my open mouth. It drips off my tongue, dribbling down my chin. I breathe hard, a drip of saliva, mine and his mixed together, falls to my chest, followed by another, then another. My mouth waters the longer I hold it open, desperately needing to swallow. My eyes begin to glaze over, my vision clouding as the sky above us starts to do the same. Hunter continues to squeeze my jaw, his eyes locked on the mess now running down the valley between my breasts. His hold on my hair the only thing holding me up, he pushes his thigh back between my legs, hiking the skirt of my flowy dress up.

I want to say his name. To get his attention. To bring his focus back to me. But I don't want to close my mouth. To ruin this dangerous game that we're playing, whatever it might be. I shudder when he releases my jaw, confident in knowing I won't break the rules.

Never Hunter's.

My mouth hangs open, tongue pushed out, as his fingers glide down the front of my throat, slipping through the mess I've made. A strangled sound escapes his throat as his fingers reach my chest. His rough fingertips drumming over my protruding bones, he swirls our saliva around, slowly dragging his fingers up and down my chest. I whine, the sound thick in my throat as I try not to splutter. Hunter's attention snaps to my eyes, his fingers stilling on my chest. Thunder rumbles in the distance, heavy clouds rolling in, matching ones forming in Hunter's dark eyes. Carefully, he untangles his fingers from my hair, combing it back behind my ear, he cups my cheek, his other hand splaying over my chest.

"Close your mouth, and swallow. Me. Down."

I don't know why, but I hesitate. His voice so low and smooth, the sound rolling up and out of his chest. It hits me like a caress, a heavy handed one. A tear slips from the corner of my right eye, he catches it on his thumb, my mouth still open, his gaze on the moisture at the tip of his thumb. Saliva continues to dribble down my chin, my throat. His thumb sweeps over my cheekbone, his eyes very, very slowly coming back to mine. I don't risk looking away from him at all. His tongue drags across his bottom lip, his thumb pressing into my cheek.

"Swallow."

One word and I'm ruined. My insides flip-flop, my heart hammers uncontrollably, trying to break free from the boned tomb it lies in. His thumb stroking over the apple of my cheek, he gazes down at me, those dreamy dark eyes of mere minutes ago consumed by shadows. Thunder clouds rolling up above us, a drop of rain hitting my cheek. I blink. Swallow. Lick my lips. And he's on me.

Hunter's teeth smash into my own, his hands holding me to his chiselled body so tightly I can't breathe. I don't want to. I don't want to do anything that might disturb what it is we're doing here. Hunter's lips mash against mine, his teeth clamping down on my bottom lip. My hands laid against his chest, trapped between us, and all I want to do is hit him for the savage way his mouth attacks me. But I want him to keep kissing me too. A war rages inside my head, my body, and I forget where I am, who I am. I feel like I'm floating and drowning all at once and its dizzying, intoxicating.

I bite back.

Hunter's tongue lashes against my mouth, pressing

against my closed lips, demanding entrance. I part my lips, claw his chest, both hands, nails tearing at his t-shirt. His tongue delves into my mouth, long, quick licks of his tongue. Consuming every inch of me, like he's never tasted anything better. My tongue slides along his, and he growls into my mouth, the sound rumbling its way up his body, vibrating through his firm chest. I feel it, in my fingers, the clammy palms of my hands.

My soul.

I force my tongue into his mouth, battling against his, tasting him right back. He clings to me harder, encouraging me to devour him. His fingers scrape against my sides, bunching my thin dress, the cotton seams creaking as he mauls me.

Everything about Hunter is animal.

He's gone, and in his place something primal.

Feral.

Wild.

Devastating.

I climb my hands up to the round neck of his t-shirt, my tongue still warring with his, my teeth and lips attacking him back. I curl my bony fingers beneath the high neck of his shirt, tearing it down, my nails dragging across his skin. He hisses into my mouth, biting down on my tongue. I claw him harder, gouging and digging my nails into his hot flesh. I taste copper, and I'm sure he does too, but I don't stop. The thin fabric knotted in my fists tears as I put pressure on it. I dig my nails into him, cutting and grazing as I rip it down the centre.

Rain patters against the top of my head, I'm

burning so hot, I don't know how the drops aren't evap-
orating as they hit my fiery flesh.

Hunter bites down harder, my tongue feeling like it's
going to tear free from my mouth when he stops. His
tongue licking over it, he sucks, *hard*, and I shiver. My
short nails mutilating his beautiful, tanned skin. I've seen
Hunter shirtless a few times. Always in the dark, shadowed, but still lit up enough beneath the moonlight we
so often find ourselves in, to be able to admire him.
Everything about Hunter is darkness, but I feel his lure.
Something inside of me tries to rip free of my skeleton
every time he's around. An undeniable pull that makes
me want to cling onto him and never let go.

I'm possessed by him, completely and utterly
consumed, my soul tears away from my spine trying to
reach him, even as his fingers press deeper into my
chest. The bones creaking beneath his weight.

I'm lost.

He devours me.

I want him to stop, at the same time I want more.

To feel his skin on mine, his fingers on my flesh, his
tongue, his lips, teeth.

I want to claw my way inside of him, meld our
bodies together, let him consume me until I'm nothing
left without him. He makes me want to hurt and to feel
and I almost want to die. Let his tongue poison me, fill
my veins with something that is all his and his alone.

Hunter draws back, the lower half of my face wet.
He licks up my chin, the tip tickling my bottom lip, he
drags it across my jaw. Licking and lapping his way

across my face. His hands roam, gliding down my back, he curls them in, tips of his fingers grinding against the bone discs in my spine. He sucks my earlobe into his mouth, nibbling the soft flesh.

His voice in my ear.

"Run."

I draw back from him, crane my neck, squint up at him as rain coats my skin, running through my hair. His teeth sink into his bottom lip. His eyes roving all over my slick face, eycing the tracks from his tongue, our spit, the cold rain. His gaze flickers over the top of my head for a second, towards the forest, the marsh. Releasing his bottom lip, he glances down at me, peering at me with his dark eyes. He runs his tongue over his lips, the bottom, then the top. A sinister grin working its way to his face.

"Run."

CHAPTER 12
HUNTER

This time she doesn't hesitate.

This time she runs.

Like a horse at the races, bolting out of the starting gate, she turns and sprints away. I watch her rush through the meadow, thigh-length, golden hair whipping behind her like glittering streamers. Floaty white dress like a breaking wave behind her. I watch her go, dark storm clouds rolling in. My cock so fucking hard I can hardly breathe.

I just had my first kiss and I know that I'll never attempt to kiss anyone else ever again.

No one but her.

I tear my eyes away from her as she sprints through the edge of the dense forest. Into the trees. I don't want to catch her if I can't hunt her down first. It would ruin this hazardous game we're playing. I don't want to be given the prize; I want to fucking earn it. Track it, search for it, seek it out and then fucking ruin it. I'm going to destroy that beautifully misguided angel. Brutalise and torture her in every sadistic, sick little way my dark mind can summon.

I glance down, eyes on my torn t-shirt, rivulets of blood oozing slowly from my shredded skin. A smirk pricks the corner of my lips. She enjoys the pain too. It's a mutual interest. *Desire.* Her innocence piqued my interest over a fortnight ago and now I'm too entangled. Unable to let her go. I can't get her mismatched gaze out of my fucking head. I don't think I'd be able to forget about her if I drilled into my own fucking skull and popped a bullet between my eyes. I've broken every fucking rule I ever set in place for myself. I wanted to stay away from people, keep myself hidden away from the oddities of the world that I find so interesting. And then the Devil himself sent one into my fucking house.

I can't seem to punish myself enough for it, no matter what I do.

So instead, *instead*, I'm going to punish *her* for it.

My perfect little Gracie.

I stare up at the sky, fingers dragging through the blood on my chest. The raindrops increasing in speed and size, falling heavily against my face, until they're drenching me. My hair saturated, I push it back, sweeping it off my face with my hand. I strip off my t-shirt, heaving it up over my head, leaving the tattered scrap at my feet.

Sucking in a deep breath, I fill my lungs with cool air and start forward. My boots marching me across the field, the horses already beneath a copse of trees. I cross the meadow, the yellow buttercups closed up without the sunlight, hiding from the dark. I sweep across the overgrown grass, a funnelled-out trail from Grace's bare feet. A road map to her starting point. I hit the tree line and pause, raking my fingers back through my soaked hair, listening. I cock my head, close my eyes. Thrown off by the fact that when I suck in a deep breath, stick out my tongue, tasting the air, I realise trying to catch her scent will never work. Grace *is* the forest. An embodiment of everything I already love; honeysuckle, leafy ferns in the height of summer, their sticky leaves masking everything around them. A sweet woodsy undercurrent of *something* entirely all her own.

The girl has been sent from the skies to test me.

Grace was created in a special corner of hell for me.

A fallen angel, banished from heaven, risen from the fiery pits of hell, wings formed of ashes, lungs full of smoke.

An enthralling depravity, angelic white skin, a halo of golden hair, a tainted, twisted soul. Something cold and menacing lurking behind those conflicting-coloured eyes. A fiery hazel handcrafted by the Devil. A glacial blue gifted by God himself. A contradiction sent to me. To test me. Punish me. Tempt me.

"Oh, little sister, I'm going to find you," I call out sinisterly, my voice low but loud.

I crack my knuckles, right hand and then the left, stepping into the trees, their wide, full branches somewhat shielding the forest floor from the rain. The wind whistles around me, through the trees, an eerie chill sending goosebumps smattering over my exposed flesh. My tight-fitting jogging bottoms soaked through, sticking to my thighs. I work my way through the long grass, my boots almost silent. My eyes quickly adjust to the darkness, the storm clouds low and rumbling overhead, giving the woods a nighttime feel despite it only being around midday.

"Gracieeeee," I call out again, listening for the rustle of leaves, the swish of grass, a flinch.

Nothing.

I wander through the trees for a while, moving quietly towards the stream, gravel disturbed, a single footprint at the edge of the water. I take my time, listening to the calming rainfall, the birds having fallen silent. Thunder rocks the trees, a flash of lightning, a strong gust of wind. I cock my head, a fallen tree, covered by neon green moss. The bark rotting, hollowed out by insects, beetles, larvae. Spying a piece of white fabric, I bite into my bottom lip so hard I taste copper as I silently approach. I fill my lungs with a deep, mind-clearing breath, my entire body thrumming with anticipation. I almost smile as I suddenly drop low, scooping at the edge of white, tugging on it so sharply I nearly fly backwards as it easily pulls free. It's just a torn edge, I realise. A piece of cotton dress snared in the jagged bark.

"Grace, I know you're out here," I sing-song teasingly.

Prey always tastes better after a chase, fear seasoning its blood.

I grind my teeth, squeeze the fabric in my closed fist, nails digging into my palm. I bring it to my nose, inhale, hold my breath, exhale, close my eyes, inhale. I get nothing. But on the breeze, even though it's been dampened down by the rain. I smell it. My eyes snap open.

French lavender.

Pocketing the fabric, I try hard to not speed up, to stay calm, to take my time. But adrenaline spikes wildly, making it difficult. It floods my veins, my heart pumping it around my body at a wicked pace. My chest heaves with breaths as my steps get faster, my boots squelching in the marsh. I'm nearing the clearing, wild garlic and French lavender in full bloom so late in the season, when I see a flash of white dart through the shadows.

I run.

Racing through the open space, her hair and dress simultaneously waving at me like a white flag of surrender. Taunting me. I pump my arms, running at her at full speed. My lungs scream, my boots suctioning in the mud with every step, like the very forest is trying to hold me back. Keep me from my prize.

I laugh.

The sound roaring up my throat, a sickening hiss between my bared teeth. Her bare feet and light weight give her the advantage, but she's got too much to grab a hold of. The fabric of her mud smeared dress, the bottom hem of it snared and torn, whips out behind her. Her three-feet of hair taunting me like fraying rope. She hops over an exposed tree root, the ground uneven as the earth starts to incline, I lunge.

I launch myself through the air as her feet lift off the ground in an attempted jump, my arms flying out in front of me. Fingers grasping onto the ends of her hair, I yank her head back against my chest, the back of her skull colliding with my collarbone as I throw myself into her. I cup her face in my hand, my other arm banding around her waist as we hit the ground, twisting us in the air so she hits the ground first, back into the sludge. I land on top of her, an *oomph* from her lungs, a grunt from her chest. I collapse on top of her. Not trying to be gentle.

I don't care if I hurt her.

I want to.

Need to.

I grab her hands, crossing her wrists, locking them above her head in one of mine, elongating her lithe little body. Other hand fisting the hair at the side of her face, yanking it away from her scalp as I slam her head down into the mud. I lift my chest from hers, my legs shifting to either side of her thighs, knees in the sludge. Straddling her, my dick straining against my joggers, grinding into her pelvic bone, so fucking close to the warm, wet place it wants to be buried inside of. Grace squirms beneath me, her pelvis rocking into my steel cock as she tries to slip away. The hand fisting the wispy hairs around her face, my knuckles sinking into the mud, I wrench her head back further. Her neck arching, baring her throat, her chest lifting from the ground, thrusting her breasts towards me as I let my hand sink into the marsh beneath our bodies.

She's breathing hard, her chest heaving with uncontrolled breaths that match mine. Fire screams through my veins, blood roaring in my ears, my eyes home in on the striking pulse in her neck. Thumping beneath her delicious, ice-white skin and I lose it.

I drop my full weight onto her, my fingers grinding the bones in her delicate wrists as my grip intensifies. I lash my tongue over her pulse, working my way up and over her jaw, I bite along the bone, nipping hard. She whimpers, trying to hold it back, but I swallow the sound. My lips finding hers, she works with me for a moment, her tongue gliding into my mouth, along my tongue, long teasing licks. Suddenly realising what she's doing, she bites into my lip, fighting me.

I smile against her mouth, despite her teeth driving hard into my lip, her tooth pricking a hole, copper tinging our kiss. I lick over her teeth. She releases my lip; I bite down on hers. She tries to pull away from me. Tugging on her head, tearing at her hands, trying to claw the back of my hand. I hold her tighter, bite her harder, teeth tearing into her fleshy bottom lip. I suck her blood into my mouth, gathering it on my tongue before letting go. Going still, she gapes up at me. Blood dribbling down her chin and mine, mismatched eyes wide, lips parted, I spit into her mouth.

She blinks.

Once.

Twice.

She spits back.

She watches silently. Her saliva mixed with mine,

our blood, hits my cheek. Letting it slide down my face, my tongue lapping at it as it reaches the corner of my mouth, I smile.

Then she fights.

She throws her head side to side, thick gold strands snapping free from her scalp, tangling around my fingers like spider's silk. Her body thrashing beneath me with every ounce of strength she has, creating the most decadent friction between us. I groan, grinding my hips against her. She stills. Chest heaving, she glares at me. I drop my forehead to hers, sharing breath.

"*Grace,*" I whisper her name against her lips.

I feel her relax beneath me, finally allowing her body to sink down into the boggy earth. I slowly lift my head from hers, my face still so close. I unknot my fingers from her hair, my eyes locked on hers the entire time, carefully, I smooth the wild strands back from her face. Rain hitting my bare back, knees squelching as they sink further into the mud. I ghost my hand down the front of her body, fingertips gliding over her bare chest, barely covered breasts, down her concave belly. The thin fabric of her white dress beneath my hand, my eyes boring into hers, I fist the skirt, thrust it up between us, exposing her to me. She doesn't move, doesn't blink. *Breathe.*

I glance down, groaning as I do, finding her bare, my teeth assaulting my bottom lip.

"Where are your knickers, little sister?" I hush in the space between us.

I push her dress up further, to the side, bunching it

up out the way. Releasing her hands hesitantly, I flick my gaze between her eyes. She keeps her hands where they are, crossed at the wrists, silent communication strong between us. She swallows, teeth scoring her lip. A mixture of our blood on her chin. I push up onto my hands, pulling my legs between hers. I suck the exposed skin of her chest, the low, square neckline giving me easy access. I run my tongue over her, the tip tracing the blue and green veins beneath her translucent skin, I follow them like rivers on a map. Pulling her dress down, I squeeze my eyes shut tightly for a second, inhale through my nose, dropping my mouth to her breasts. No bra, just blemish free skin and dusty pink nipples, already pulled into sharp little points.

God, she's so perfect.

I take one between my teeth, sucking hard, pulling as much of her flesh into my mouth as I can, fingers and thumb tweaking the other, I switch between the two. Dipping lower, my teeth biting the fabric between us, lifting it up higher. My tongue glides over her flat belly, dipping into her bellybutton, swirling down lower. I kiss her hip bone, my mouth sloppily pressing open mouthed kisses along her pelvis, until I reach the other, pressing a kiss there too.

My hands holding onto her tiny waist, fingers digging in. Sliding my palms down her sides, over her hips, to the insides of her thighs. I curl my arms beneath her legs, holding onto her like I'll never let her go. And I won't. Not just in this moment, but from here on out this girl is fucking mine.

I glance up, her eyes looking down her nearly naked body, instantly locking on mine as I sharply part her knees. I make sure she's watching me and bury my face between her thighs.

I breathe in deep, groaning, inhaling her sweet scent.

"You smell so fucking good, baby girl," I rasp, a whimper escaping her throat.

Curling her thigh over my forearm, trapping it in the crook of my elbow, I part her wet lips with my finger and thumb, exposing her to the cold air. Dragging myself in closer, I keep my eyes on hers as I open my mouth, press the flat of my tongue over her clit, and lap at her. Her taste explodes on my tongue, sweet and tangy, floral. I groan deeply, dragging her in against my mouth, I work my tongue over her. Longer, bolder licks. I dip my tongue into her tight little hole, gathering her arousal, dragging it up to her clit. Smothering her in it, my lips, chin, cheeks. Everything covered in her as I plunge my face into her cunt.

She cries out, my tongue gliding bottom to top, up and down the length of her pussy, I apply pressure, then pull away. Her hips gyrate against my face, her knees attempting to lock me in place. My hands hold her open. She shakes under my assault, her hands slapping down on the top of my head. Fingers knotting in the strands, pulling on the roots, pushing down on my head. Like she wants to tear me away and push me in deeper all at once.

Her taste, her scent, her soft, almost silent, little whimpers as she grinds her clit against my tongue.

Everything overwhelming my senses. I cover her with my mouth. My tongue sinking into her, I fuck her with it, my thumb finding her clit. Rubbing her in fast, tight circles, my tongue plunging in and out of her as deep as I can go, her nails clawing at my scalp, she explodes.

Her hips slam into my face, lifting off the ground, her legs firmly trapped in my arms, her shoulders pushing her up. I continue lapping at her, swallowing down everything she rewards me with. Finally, she relaxes in my arms, shaking violently, I place her legs down, my body still between her thighs. I glance up, her eyes still on me, I climb up her body, until my hips are level with hers and I can stare down into her eyes.

Her beautiful eyes shining despite the shadows. Her lips parted, hot breath puffing into the cool air between us. I cup her face, my thumb smoothing over her cheekbone. My lips find hers; I kiss her gently, carefully. Exploring her mouth with my tongue in a slow sensual kiss. I tell her everything in this kiss. How she makes me feel alive for the first time in my fucking life. How she thinks she's strange but she's perfect to me, in every weird and wonderful fucking way.

I want to consume her.

I'm going to consume her.

And she'll want me to.

I don't want her to think about anything but me and what I can give her for the rest of her life. I'm going to bury myself inside of her so deep she'll feel me imprinted inside of her for the rest of her fucking existence. And every time I think she needs a reminder; I'm going to give her one.

"*Hunter*," she breathes the word between us like a prayer and my already hard dick turns to steel.

Keeping my eyes on hers, I push up onto my knees, between her spread thighs. Shove the waistband of my joggers down, over my hips, my hard cock bobbing free, the tip already beaded with pre-cum. I fist myself, squeeze the base, run my hand up my length, drag the pre-cum around the crown with my thumb. I breathe deep, the animal inside me roaring to tear her in two, I try to control myself. I bite my lip, pop it free, think of the chase.

The rain pelts down now, hammering, spearing my bare back like drops of acid. My nostrils flare as Grace looks up at me, one warm hazel eye, the dark freckle beneath, the other wide eye an ice blue. She looks at me like I hung the moon. And in this moment, I know I'd tear it from the fucking sky for her if she wanted me to. Fuck the rest of the world. Let it descend into chaos around us. I'm going to give this delicately, unusual girl every fucking thing she ever wanted and everything she didn't know she did.

I'm going to kill anyone that dares look upon this heavenly creature.

I swallow hard, my heart bursting at the seams, blood, hot like lava, thrums through my veins at a rapid pace. I breathe in, focus my gaze on her, fist my dick, dip my head. My mouth hovering just above hers.

"This is going to hurt, baby girl," I whisper against her lips and slam my way inside her.

She arches up at my sudden intrusion. The tight walls of her cunt squeezing me so tightly I forget how to fucking breathe. I grit my teeth, never having felt anything like this before. I've imagined thrusting into her, ripping through her, driving my dick deep inside of her, where no one's ever been before. Where no one but me will ever go again. Just in the same way I will never stray. This is already it for me. I can feel it. Feel her. Our connection. Imagining it all those nights was nothing like this.

She claws at my chest, gouging the already torn flesh, I slam my palm down onto her chest, forcing her down into the marsh. My other hand lifting her right hip, I grip her thigh, curl her leg around my lower back. Slide myself out of her, brutally thrust back in, all the way to the hilt.

Knowing this isn't going to last anywhere near long enough, I stare down at her, tears streaming from the corners of her eyes. She winces beneath my weight on her chest, her lips parted, her heart punching against my palm. Her rain slicked skin so soft beneath my hand, the bones of her ribcage digging into my fingers. I press down on her chest, bend my elbow, lower my chest to hers. One arm trapped between us, she pulls the other free, cups my face. Caresses my cheek, her thumb on my already split top lip. I want to close my eyes, keep them open, pull out, push back in. But I don't do any of those things. I slide my hand up her thigh, calf still around my waist. I splay my hand in the mud beside her head.

Her pussy pulses around me, so hot, and so fucking wet, I'm intoxicated. Drugged to the high heavens, everything about her possessing me. The pull she has, my soul ripping away from my skeleton to get to her. I groan as her thumb nail savagely tears the scab away, blood dripping from my split lip, steadily dripping onto her pale face. Her eyes drop to my mouth, her thumb smearing the thick crimson over my lips, across my cheek. She glides her thumb and then her finger through the mess, wiping my blood up my face. It splatters against hers and I'm certain I've never seen anything more fucking beautiful.

I pull out of her tight little cunt, peer down between us, my dick slick, that too, smeared in crimson, glistening with her juices. My tip at her entrance, her blood on my rock-hard cock, mine on her face. I forcefully slam my way back inside her, grunting with the suffocating grip she has around me, when she backhands me across the face. I blink, she claws my neck, lurches forward, bites into my arm still on her chest. Her eyes on mine, I rip my arm out of her mouth, blood down my arm, blood on her teeth, she grins at me. For the first fucking time since I've known her, she grins at me and it's nothing short of feral.

I force my forearm across her throat, my weight pushing her deeper and deeper into the mud, her hands come up, straight for my throat. Her fingers close around my neck, I tilt my head, peer down at her. Her lips turn up at the corners, the smallest, softest, most genuine smile I've ever been blessed with, and she squeezes. Her fingers close around my throat, and she puts *everything* into her hold on me. My air cuts off and I lose it.

I pound into her, both her legs curling around my back, heels of her feet digging into my arse. My arm across her throat, my other hand on her waist, fingertips driving into her ribs, I pummel into her. My dick smashing in and out of her at a brutal pace. My eyes bulge, my lungs burning without air. Her pussy clamps down around me, her orgasm ripping through her and then she's clawing at my throat, and I'm coming. I thrust into her so hard our pelvises smack together, hips colliding, bones bruising with the force as I bury myself inside of her, hold myself there. Her cunt sucks me in, her body shakes and trembles beneath me. Her hands drop from my clawed neck. Blood beneath her nails, on her hands. She lays her palms against my chest, her fingers sliding over the torn skin, through the mess of blood.

I breathe hard, my chest heaving, heart hammering. My face stings, my lip throbbing as blood continues to leak from it. I sit up, still inside of her, reach forward, grasp her arms and lift her into my lap. She winces as she straddles my thighs, my arm at her back, hand at the nape of her neck. I tilt her head back until her eyes are on me, blood smeared all over her face, mud caked in the back of her hair. I'm positive I've never seen anything more perfect. I lean in, my lips hovering over hers, I let her decide. I wait. She moves in, her lips melding to mine. Electricity hums through me, my muscles aching, bones vibrating. Blood thrumming with heat, I squeeze her to me, my other hand on her cheek, fingers splayed over her ear. I shove her hair away from her face, our chests pressed together.

Kissing her back, she sinks her tongue into my mouth, slowly, probing mine, I let her lead, taste me. I slide my tongue over hers, gently sucking on it, she kisses me harder, her hands on my chest stroking instead of clawing. Her cold fingers make my skin sting, but I welcome her touch. She leans back slightly, breaking our kiss, her tongue sliding out to lick her lips, my cock already hardening inside of her at the sight. She rests her forehead against mine, her eyes sliding closed.

"Hunter," she breathes against me, a chill rushing up my spine, tingling in my scalp. She swallows, takes a soft breath. "Again."

CHAPTER 13
GRACE

Hunter holds me to his warm body, clutching me close to his chest, his chin rests on the top of my head as we both breathe hard. Everything aches, my muscles, my bones, my teeth. The space between my thighs still full of him even as he softens again. I'm wet, from both of us, it tingles. I feel raw and overly sensitive, and like I might cry but I don't know why. I shiver, my teeth chattering as he holds me protectively to him, his arms around me like he'll never let anyone take me away from him. They'd have to pry his cold dead arms off of me before he'd willingly let go. A sob gets caught in my throat, I bite my lip, holding it in.

The rain is still falling, less now, but it's bitter, my body trembling, goosebumps erupting over my flesh from the cold breeze and the freezing rain. Hunter pulls out of me, slides me off of his lap, lifts me to my feet, hold firm on my waist, then he stands too. He brushes my hair back from my face, his two big hands carefully holding the sides of my face, his touch gentle. So unlike us, but it still pushes warmth through me. His dark eyes on mine makes my stomach drop and my heart flutter. I feel hot when he hurts me, when I hurt him back. I feel safe and wanted and I don't know what to do about it. But when he's like this, I don't understand it. But I know one thing is certain.

This is temporary.

Despite the fact that Hunter is my stepbrother.

And this is wrong.

I'm going to be sent back.

Far away from here.

Alone.

I drop my gaze. My heart seizing in my chest, that little creature inside biting down on the dying organ. Hunter told me in the kitchen that there isn't a creature inside there. He never told me what it was though. I stare at my feet, sinking into the marsh, mud sucking me into the earth. I wonder if I should let it. Perhaps it will hurt less than whatever happens from here. I sweep my hands down the front of my dress, mud and blood weighing it down, making it feel as heavy as my insides. Hunter tilts my head back, my eyes still down. I can't look at him. Even as his cum slides down the insides of my thighs, and I should feel, well, anything but what I'm feeling right now, I don't know how to look up at him without letting my tears slip free.

"Gracie, look at me," he whispers, his deep voice, raspy and almost silent in the air between us.

I can feel his warm breath on my face, his scent fills my nostrils, my chin wobbles. He must see it because in the next breath he crushes me to his chest, my skull secured against his pounding heart. His large hand on the back of my head, one stroking down my back. We stand like that until I give in. Until my arms slide up his sides, loop around his back, hands linked together. He exhales. Like he's been holding his breath, waiting on me, waiting for me to give in.

Like he can read my thoughts, feel what I feel, he says, "there's no creature inside of there, baby girl. What that feeling is, when your heart aches and twists inside your chest. And you can't breathe without it spiking with pain. That's what it is, Gracie. It's pain. Not from a physical pain. An emotional pain. When someone calls you strange-" I flinch, he smooths down my hair. "When someone calls you nasty names, when they hit you, taunt you, pick on you because of your beautiful eyes. That's on them, baby, that's on them. It's not you, it's never been you. You're perfect, Grace. So fucking perfect and innocent that it calls to the evil in this world, and it tries to twist you into something else, tries to tarnish you and your heart."

Hunter pulls away, his big hands back on either side of my face.

"But I won't let them, baby girl. I won't let anyone fucking near you ever a-fucking-gain. I'll kill anyone that even thinks about looking at you. You're mine now and I'm never going to let anything get to you ever again. I swear it. I'll die before I do. For you, Grace, you mean everything to me."

His thumbs swipe beneath my eyes, collecting the tears I didn't know escaped, I pull in a trembling breath. My hands tighten around him, warmth flowing through my chest now. A chest that doesn't have a stowaway creature locked inside of it. I feel lighter, like I can breathe without weights inside my lungs making it difficult.

"You're safe with me, baby girl. You'll always be safe with me, Gracie."

Tyson and Duke lay their big furry bodies on the floor either side of the bath, keeping us safe inside of Hunter's bathroom. The walls and floor a deep green marble. *Jade.* He had said. I thought it was just a pretty name, but apparently, it's the name of a pretty colour too. We showered first, in our clothes, then without our clothes. Then Hunter filled this huge tub with warm bubbly water. It's bigger than the one in my room upstairs, a room I now know once belonged to my oldest brother Thorne. I lay back against Hunter's lean body, his muscles hard against me. My bum sat between his open thighs, his bent knees on either side, bracing me in. His big hands on my belly, his fingers tracing patterns on my skin beneath the hot water. My head against his chest.

Steam fills the room, my eyes slip closed, I curl my arms beneath the water, up and around Hunter's thighs, my fingers dancing across the inside of his legs. I breathe in deeply, my lungs expanding fully in what feels like forever. I hum beneath my breath, sinking further into the water, against Hunter's big body. His hands on my belly slow their movements until they're not moving at all. One sliding up, cupping my breast, tweaking my nipple. I breathe out, his other hand sliding down my body. I turn my head up into him, press my face into the crook of his neck, breathing him in. His hand slips between my tender thighs, his finger sliding through my wet slit. I arch my back, his thumb finding my clit, his finger slips inside of me.

"You're so fucking wet, four times and you're still so wet," he groans appreciatively.

The warm water, the hot heat from his finger slowly working in and out of me, the circular motion from his thumb, it takes me no time at all. I screw my eyes shut, my breath held, muscles pulled taut, I let go. His finger slows, his thumb lazily rolling over my clit, his other hand finds my face. He tilts my head up, brings his lips to mine and kisses me until I'm dizzy. I lap at the split in his top lip, gently suckle it into my mouth, cleaning it up where it still weeps a little. His teeth nip at my bottom lip, not trying to hurt this time. I lift my arm from the water, foamy bubbles rushing down my wet skin, my hand finds his face, fingers teasing his straight black hair, thumb on his square jaw. He kisses me and I kiss him back and I hurt inside not knowing how long this is going to last.

Hunter washes my hair, soaps up my body, rinses me clean and tends to my wounds. His are worse. Jagged claw marks indent his usually flawless skin. I'm sat up on the counter beside the sink, in too many big towels. One twisted up on top of my head, two wrapped around my small body, one draped over my shoulders so I don't get cold.

Hunter stands before the basin, a towel tied low on his waist, his chiselled abs on display, a deep V between his hips. He leans into the mirror, applying cream to the deep slices in his chest, I watch him methodically coat each one, a thin greasy sheen appearing over them, almost highlighting them. I swallow, look down at my hands, my short nails are clean now, but they weren't, they were filled with mud and a sticky red substance. A piece of Hunter. He scrubbed my nails, my hair, my skin, until I was pink and clean all over. I glance up, looking at him from beneath my lashes as he recaps the ointment, places it inside the mirrored cabinet. I can see the red mark upon his cheek, the other side to his fading black eye.

"I put that there," I tell him, his eyes snapping to mine.

His brow creases, a twitch in his jaw. I fiddle with my hands, my fingers clicking as I clench and unclench my fists.

"You did," he affirms almost proudly.

I drop my gaze to his chest.

"I did that too," I nod my head in his direction, eyes still locked on the shiny wounds.

"Yep," he pops the 'P', seemingly unaffected.

"Is that… what we did, is it…" I lick my lips, my tongue dry, I blink quickly.

"Normal?" he rumbles, the word leaving him with obvious distaste.

"Yes," I whisper, my eyes on my hands.

He turns to face me, one hand splayed over the counter, the other on his jaw. He thumbs his lips, wiping at the bottom one, studying me.

"Is that what you want, Grace?" he asks, and I peer up at him, confused by his question. "To be *normal*," he clarifies, and I blink slowly, unsure of my answer. "It's okay to say yes, you can tell me anything," he says quietly, his hand coming to my cheek.

It's the warmest I ever feel, his hands on my face.

"I just want to be…"

"Be?" he coaxes.

Moving in closer, he parts my legs, steps between them, plants his hands either side of my thighs.

"I don't know," I tell him honestly.

I look up into his dark eyes, swirling like little galaxies. I reach out, my finger smoothing over his dark eyebrow, the one with the jagged scar through the arch. I trace it lightly, admiring the strong masculine features of his face. Straight nose, plump lips, sharp, square jaw. His thick, straight hair that sometimes covers one eye. He pushes it back, but it falls forward.

"You don't need to know right now, we've got all the time in the world, little sister."

My lips curl a little, on one side, it's not a smile, but I wish it were. I think about never seeing this face again and my insides ache, like some of my parts stop working for a moment.

"Why are you so sad, baby girl?"

Hunter slides his hand around my throat, his fingers stroking up the sides of my neck. I relax forward, his fingers tighten, and I feel better, leaning on him. Letting him hold me up. I swallow, shake my head, look up at him.

His thumb strokes over my pulse. He leans in, pressing his forehead to mine, his eyes flicker between my own, so close he's blurry but I breathe him in, smell daisies, moss, the stream. And I exhale, long and slow. He kisses me, pressing his lips to mine, then the top of my head, he holds me close, and I can breathe.

I can finally breathe.

CHAPTER 14
HUNTER

Weeks pass by, Grace sleeps in my bed, holds my hand, I feed her up, with Rosie's help of course. Rosie teaches her how to braid her hair. I start teaching her how to read, it's slow going but she's learning. She loves books. Horrors, actually. I've read and re-read *'The Shining'* to her countless times, but her reactions are always the same, shock, surprise, intrigue.

Fear.

My heart swells so hard when I look at her beautiful face, colour in her cheeks, that it makes me want to fucking kill Eleanor. But I refrain. My dad keeps her busy, out of the house, away from me. *Her.* My brothers come home regularly, getting to know her, keeping her busy whilst I'm working, in the room connected to my bedroom. The one I stare at when she falls asleep in my arms every night, the dogs curled up on the end of the bed, her feet tucked beneath Tyson. Anxiety rides me hard, at her finding out the truth and hating me for it, it leaves me restless and irritable.

She stops taking her cocktail of poison pills, which Archer discovered weren't actually intended to treat anything. Just keep her docile and compliant. Silent and sleepy. She's better now.

Happy.

But still sad.

A dark cloud shadows every moment we share, but I can't work out what it is. She tells me it's nothing, that she feels better, *good*. And I want to believe her, but I don't. She hasn't wandered off without me, not since our first time together. Which there have been many, many more of. I hurt her. She hurts me back. Like a cyclone, a mess of passion and pain, we can't keep our hands off of each other.

I wander into the stables finding Grace already inside Lady's stall. Standing at her side, her long twin braids hang over one slim shoulder, swinging gently against her as she bushes Lady down. One hand splayed against her shiny black coat, the other sweeping the brush down her side. I lean against the open door. Lady huffing through her nose, nodding her head at me. I cross my arms over my chest, peer at her through the dark hair hanging over my eye. Methodically, she brushes Lady's coat exactly as I showed her, every sweep of her hand, the direction of her hair. Everything perfect and to the exact letter. Grace is slowly letting go of needing rules. But it's hard, she can't seem to make decisions for herself, doesn't understand why we do and don't do things certain ways. But she's getting there slowly. We're being patient. It's all I could ask for.

"What you doing, baby girl?" I finally call out, my head tilting, taking in her arse covered in tight cream jodhpurs.

She doesn't startle, continues to brush Lady.

"You're taking me out riding," she tells me, and I chuckle.

"Oh, I am?" I raise an eyebrow, her head slowly rising to look at me.

"Yes."

I laugh, uncross my arms and wander in. My hand going straight for Lady's nose, I run my hand down the flat of her face, her big brown eyes watching me, wondering if I brought her any mints. I didn't, she would have sniffed them out immediately, but she's still hopeful. Grace straightens, placing the oval brush into the bucket. She walks forward, her arms finding my neck, she squeezes her body against me, my dick already hard, I groan. My free arm goes around her lower back, clutching her to me, I kiss the top of her head, the tip of her nose.

"I like your pants," I tell her, grabbing her arse.

"They're called, um, they're something for riding horses in," she tells me, I bite into my lip, holding in my laugh, but I shake with it anyway.

She slaps her hand against my chest, pulling away to peer up at me.

"Don't laugh," she frowns, only making me laugh harder.

"Jodhpurs," I chuckle.

"I did know that," she huffs and I smirk.

"I know," I nod, pulling her back into me, needing to keep her close.

"So, will you take me?" she whispers against my chest.

"I will, get your boots on."

I clip reins onto Lady's bridle, the only piece of equipment she doesn't mind wearing. She won't be saddled and that's okay, I prefer to ride without. I lead her outside, Grace sits on a small wooden step, pulling on her left boot. Lady scuffs her foot into the dry earth, we've had no rain for weeks, everything drying out. The weather is unseasonably hot for the start of October, but it's making up for a wet September, I suppose. Grace stands up, looking up at me, Lady's back level with my chest. She's eighteen-hands, I'm six-foot-four. Grace is not. I laugh lightly as she looks up at me, her mismatched eyes wide, curiosity thick in the air between us.

I wink at her, her cheeks turning pink, she drops her gaze. I lift her under the arms, she lifts her leg up and over without instruction. I place the reins in her hands, then pull myself up behind her. Lady takes an eager step forward, ready to gallop. I slide forward, my thighs clamping around Grace, she leans back into me, my arms going around her sides. I slip my hands over hers, around the reins. Rest my chin down on her shoulder.

"You ready?"

She nods against me, and I squeeze my legs. Lady

starts forward, a slow, gentle pace. We wander through the wildflowers, the hot sun beaming down on us. We pass the old waterwheel, round the house and head off towards the open fields. I squeeze my thighs against Lady's sides, and she takes off. Desperate to pick up speed, she gallops, her head down, her black mane whipping out behind her. Her hooves pound across the dry ground, the grass yellowing. I grip Grace hard, keeping her safe against me. One of my hands on the reins, the other wrapping around her middle. I look down at her, her eyes wide, a small smile on her face.

"Hold on," I say in her ear, her little fists tightening on the leather.

Lady canters across the meadow, through fields of poppies, daisies and buttercups. Up and over the hills, we circle around, coming up beside the lake. I pull back on Lady's reins, she starts to slow, trotting us to the edge of the lake, she stops, dips her head forward and takes a long drink.

I shift myself and slide off her back, I reach my hand up for Grace, she slips hers into my palm, and slides herself down. I catch her, placing her onto her feet. I kneel down before her, tapping her shin with my fingers, she raises her foot, one hand resting on my shoulder. I grip the heel of her foot, tugging off her boot, then do the other, tossing them over my shoulders. I slide her socks off next, my eyes still locked on her face, she watches me. I raise my hands towards her waistband, my finger and thumb popping the button free.

She breathes in. Short, sharp pants, her plump lips

parted as she watches me slowly slide her zipper down. My hands go around her back, fingers curling beneath the high waistband, I roll them down, over the hump of her arse, down her creamy thighs. She lifts her feet, one at a time, stepping out of the ivory jodhpurs. I throw them away from us, my eyes still on hers. Her chest heaving, hands shaking at her sides. I close my eyes, my hands on her arse cheeks, I pull her into me, my nose pressed to her pussy. I suck in a deep breath, inhaling her tangy, floral scent. Her hands tangle in my hair, nails scraping softly over my scalp. I look up at her, her eyes already on me. I climb to my feet, her fingers going for the buttons on my black shirt, she pops each one free with precision. Her eyes on mine, she pushes it off my shoulders, down my arms, letting it float down to the grass. I grasp the hem of her white vest top, gather it in my hands, lift it up and over her head.

I take a step back, leaving her in nothing but her white cotton knickers. I bite my lip so hard I draw blood. I relish in the pain, I need it, to help me control myself, to stop me tearing her in two. I step backwards again, my feet taking me closer to the water. I kick my boots off, still moving, my black jeans go next, quickly followed by my black boxers. Grace's gaze drops to my dick bobbing free, hard and already glistening with pre-cum. She licks her lips, her eyes drawing back up to mine, she starts toward me, a sway to her hips that has me salivating. She doesn't even know she's doing it. What effect she has on me. The pull. The fucking *need* I have for her.

Her thumbs go to the sides of her underwear, she

pushes them down, letting them fall down her thighs. One foot steps out of them, using the other to twirl them around her ankle, she flings them at me. Her freshly shaved cunt on full display, I groan.

"D'you do that for me, little sister?" I rasp, my eyes glued to her naked body, her translucent skin glistening radiantly in the sun.

She nods silently, shyly, her twin braids covering her dusty pink nipples. I lick my lips, step into the cold water, I wait for her, the water ankle deep. She stops at the edge of the lake, her eyes peering over my head, gaze on the depths.

Lady stands on the bank, grazing on the long grass.

"I've got you," I reassure her, I take a step further back, holding my hand out.

She looks at it, her eyes flicking up to mine, I nod, extending my hand out further. She slips her delicate fingers into mine, I clasp them in my palm, and tug her gently into the water. She takes a few tender steps, I continue backward, leading her with me. She shivers as the cold water reaches her thighs, we continue deeper, water lapping at the middle of my back, I come to a stop.

"Hunter," she says quietly, nervously, unsure.

"I've got you," I promise her, watching her teeth nibble her lower lip.

I draw her into me, twisting quickly in the water. Boosting her up onto my back, she gasps as I wrap her legs around my waist. Her arms automatically going around my neck. I walk forwards, my hands on her legs until the water laps at my chin. I kick off the bottom, my arms going out before me, I swim, she squeezes me so hard I think she's cutting off my circulation, but she laughs.

It's wild and carefree and so fucking freeing, I laugh too. Her forearms locked across my throat, her thighs crushing my sides, I swim us out into the middle of the lake. Treading water, I loosen her arms, twist her around until she's on my front. I float us there for a while, just bobbing in the smooth surface of the water. I point out the direction of the house, the woods, the stables. Trying to map out the land in case she ever found herself out here alone again.

"Hunter," she whispers, her eyes on my lips, our faces close. "Don't let me go."

"I'm never letting you go, Grace."

Still clinging to my front, I swim us closer to shore, my toes brush against the bottom of the lake, sand and small stones beneath my feet. I stand, the water up to the base of my throat. I keep Grace on me, she can't stand here. I lick my lips and lean in, press a kiss to her lips, she kisses me back. Instantly parting her lips, allowing me entrance, my tongue rolls over hers, long teasing licks into her mouth. I grasp the back of her head, angling her with my hold, my tongue delving deeper. She moans, I swallow the soft sounds she makes as she grinds herself against me, her pussy grinding over my abs.

My hard cock between us, I reach down, grasping the base, lining up with her entrance, I break our kiss.

Fisting my hand in her hair, I tip her head back, forcing her to look at me.

"I'm not a good man, Grace," I confess, unsure why now is the time to divulge. "I'm not…" I swallow, my Adam's apple bobbing in my throat. "I'm not good, Gracie," I whisper.

"Hunter," she says softly, in that way that she always does, it makes my throat tighten whenever I hear it. Dropping her gaze, "I'm not good either," she tells me solemnly. "I've never been good."

I swipe loose hairs from her face, fallen free from her plaits.

"You're good to me, baby girl, you're so fucking good, Gracie."

Her eyes peer into mine, that frosty blue and fiery hazel. She searches me for the truth, trying to find the lie. Her brow creasing, she swallows. The air between us thin, it makes it hard to breathe when she looks at me like I have all the answers. Like I know everything.

Just like I know, that in a moment, when my dick is buried deep inside of her and she claws at my skin, draws blood and sucks it from her fingers. That I'm going to fist her hair, bite her throat and cut off her breath. That neither one of us are good. Not to each other. The thought chokes me, my lungs seizing, my heart thudding slow like it's flooded with poison. The bruises that I leave all over her perfect skin, the cuts and scrapes, nips and teeth marks. The puncture wounds we leave behind on each other. None of it is good. But it *feels* good. In the moment. It feels fucking good.

"I don't think…"

She trails off, her eyes going over my shoulder, out to the depths. I pinch her chin between my thumb and finger, drag her focus back to me.

"You don't think what, baby girl?"

"That I'm *good*."

"Grace, you're good to me," I tell her. "You're good to me even when you're bad," I whisper against her lips. "You're so fucking good to me."

"I am?" she questions, her eyes flicking between my own.

I nod, my tongue licking over the seam of her lips. One hand on the back of her head, the other fisting the base of my cock.

"Show me just how good you are, little sister," I hush, thrusting my steel length inside of her.

I sink my tongue into her mouth, fist her hair, pull her into me. My free hand going to her arse, I grope her flesh beneath the water. Forcing my hard cock in and out of her tight, little cunt. She pulses around me, desperately trying to adjust to my thickness. I kiss her like a savage, my teeth tearing at her lips, nipping her tongue. She rips her mouth from mine, bobbing up and down on my dick, her knees digging into my sides. Both hands gripping my shoulders, fingers curled over, nails carving into my shoulder blades. I fuck up into her, she slams herself down onto me as much as is possible beneath the clear surface of the water. I dip down, swirl my tongue over one nipple then the other, pulled into sharp little points, I suck hard, lashing my tongue over them.

She drops her forehead to the back of her hand curled over my shoulder. Turns her head into me, her lips against the side of my throat. She licks up to my ear, teeth catching the lobe. She bites down, sucking away the sting.

"Hit me," she breathes against my skin, goosebumps materialise over my cool flesh.

I slow, crane my neck back trying to look at her. My dick stilling inside her, even as she clenches her walls around me, trying to force me deeper.

"What?" I blink, certain I've misheard.

"Hit me," she whispers, and I shudder.

I lean back from her, shaking my head, when her hand whips out, cracking me across the jaw. My head flies right, my teeth aching, I flex my jaw, hearing it click. I lick my lips, turn my head back to her, the skin on my face hot.

"Hit me."

"Grace, n-"

She hits me again, this time I see stars, I blink hard, working my jaw. I turn to look at her, her hand raised, I grab her wrist, grind the bones together beneath my thick fingers.

"Stop it," I warn her, my teeth grinding, I shake my head. "No, Grace."

My voice low and threatening, she stares at me, clenches her pussy around me, my dick getting ever harder the longer she stares at me.

"*Hunter.*"

I groan at my name on her tongue, closing my eyes,

I huff out a breath through my nose. Warring with myself. I shouldn't hit her. I've *never* thought about hitting her. I don't *actually* want to hurt her.

Do I?

"Get off of me," she says almost silently, her eyes downcast.

She squirms in my hold, her free hand pushing against my chest. I tighten my grip on her body, grind the bones in her delicate wrist, gritting my teeth. She tries to break free, uncaring that we're in five and a half feet of water and she can't swim.

"Grace, stop, you don't want me to hit you, baby girl."

"I DO!" she screams at me. "DO IT!" she rips her hand free from my grip, pummels her hand against my chest.

"HIT. ME!"

My heart thuds, my lungs deflate even as I try to pull in a deep breath.

Without conscious thought my hand sails through the air, colliding so hard against her cheek I hear her neck crack as her head whips to the side. I breathe hard. My chest heaving, my eyes burning. My hand tingles. The palm of it hot, itchy beneath the skin. I heave in breath after breath. Her loose hair hiding her face from me where she leans to one side, the heat of the sun burning the top of my head, her pale shoulders pink. I should have gotten her sun cream.

I shouldn't have brought her out here.

I shouldn't have hit her.

"Gracie?" I whisper, her chest heaving, clashing with mine with every breath.

Slowly, so slowly, she lifts her head, blood on her lip, her eyes glassy, my handprint on her cheek, cherry red and glowing. She stares at me for so long I forget how to breathe. I forget my fucking dick is still hilt deep inside of her, until she rotates her hips, her cunt clenching around my cock. I grit my teeth as she starts to ride me again, her arms locking around my neck, nails clawing at my spine.

"Grace, I'm-"

"Again," she demands, using me to lift herself up, dropping herself back down onto my hard cock. "Again," she licks her lips, smearing the blood.

A cut in her cupid's bow, half a centimetre long, too long. It's swelling and I hate that I fucking love seeing it there. That I did that.

You're a sick fuck, Hunter.

Her eyes locked on mine, I start to fuck up into her, slamming myself into her as hard as I can with the resistance of the water. She bites into her top lip, sucking on the blood spilling from her face. She fills her mouth, sticks out her tongue, showing me the evidence of what I did to her. My eyes flicker between hers, drop to her tongue, back up to her eyes. I lick my lips, thrust up into her, lock my arm behind her back, my other going to her hair. I wind her braid around my fist, roping it around my knuckles until she winces at the pull in her scalp. Her mouth still open, I spit on her tongue, then lick up our mess. I plunge my tongue into her mouth, suck and swallow against her. My teeth clashing with hers, our mouths colliding. We fight each other, trying to outdo the other, my cock still slamming into her. She rears back, her lip tearing free from my teeth.

I hit her.

The palm of my hand cracks across her cheek, slamming her face to the side. I keep up my pace, getting closer and closer to coming when her hot pussy pulses around me. She straightens, readjusts her grip on me, cups my face and smiles. Blood across her pearly whites, she smiles, a real, full smile.

And I realise as she starts to come, as my dick releases deep inside of her cunt, painting the entrance of her cervix with my cum, I surrendered.

I just gave her exactly what she wanted.

I fully let go with her.

She can wield me like a weapon now if she so chooses.

I'll do anything she asks of me, no matter how fucked up it might be.

I'm gone for her.

I'm fucking in *love* with her.

And in doing so, I give her all the power.

CHAPTER 15

GRACE

My eye is swollen, and it's one of the only times I can stand to look at myself. When I have proof on my face that my Hunter really exists. That he put those beautiful strong hands on my face and made sure I wouldn't forget. That I'm not still locked up in that school, trapped inside my tiny room, bars on my windows.

I smooth the pad of my thumb over the reddening lump, on the upper part of my cheekbone. I press into it, making sure I can feel what I see, not wanting it to fade too fast. I pull the towel from my head, letting it slap to the floor, my long, wet locks soaking my back. I'm waiting for Rosie to help me get ready because we're having a party. Here, at the house. There have already been cars pulling up, people rushing in and out all day. Caterers that Rosie kept telling off and people with costumes and decorations. One man came in a tractor pulling a trailer full of pumpkins.

It's October thirtieth.

Hunter's birthday.

Apparently, it's the night before All Hallows' Eve, when people dress up as scary things and jump out at one another.

Not me, though. Archer chose my costume. He said it suited me, that I can't dress up as something scary because I'm too *good*. I haven't looked at it yet. Even though it makes my tummy ache with not knowing what it is. I've left it hidden inside the large black clothing case it came in.

I exhale, press my thumb into my reddening eye.

Hunter.

Rosie bustles into the bedroom, I hear her through the open door to my adjoining bathroom. Shuffling around, mumbling under her breath. A few minutes pass, she pokes her head around the bathroom door.

"Grace, come and sit in this chair, child!" she exclaims, her pitch high, shrill, it makes me clamp my hands over my ears.

She tuts, hurries in, grabs my elbow and tows me to the dressing table. I sit on the padded stool, clawed feet carved into the wood, an ivory cushion on the seat. Rosie eyes the mark on my cheek, but she doesn't say anything. I wouldn't tell her about my bruises the first time, other than to say I fell, she knew I lied and hasn't asked since. She pulls a brush through my hair, meticulously drying it root to tip. She sections it off, curling it using a hot tool. Plaits an array of different braids through it, pulling at the loops of some so they look messy. She calls them all different names, but she whistles as she does them, the sound more comfortable than making words. After pulling the front sections of my hair back, securing them with gold slides, she paints my face. Telling me to look this way and that, to close and open my eyes, pucker my lips and massage them together. I find the entire process draining.

By the time she's finished, the sun has set, and the moon is high in the sky. I peer up at it through my large window, fingers pressed to the cool glass. The dense forest blowing in the breeze, the usually pitch-black grounds glowing with flickering light. Jack O'Lanterns. Pumpkins with faces cut into them and a lit candle stuffed into their hollow shell where their insides used to be. Raine let me make one with him, he showed me how to scrape the gunk out with my hands. Told me I was a natural. I didn't know people were born specifically to carve pumpkins, but I don't think it's really a career I want to pursue. He chuckled; told me I was funny. It made my insides feel warm when he said that.

Rosie gasps somewhere across the room, I turn my head over my shoulder with a frown. She hasn't gasped like that since she found a Merlin Falcon in here. He had a broken wing, I was nursing him. She called Hunter; he took him back to his mother.

"Oh, *Grace*," she says in a way that has my heart pounding harder.

I turn towards her, her back to me as she leans over the bed. Wandering closer, I hear a zip, try to peer around her from where I stop in the middle of the room. I'm in a towel, my hair and make-up done, my body slathered in too many lotions to name. I bite my lip as Rosie peers over her shoulder, her eyes locked on mine, a mischievous smile on her face.

"What?" I question when my body starts to shake with not knowing.

"Come look," she jerks her head towards my made bed, "it doesn't bite, come on," she laughs when I hesitate.

My feet find their way to her, I stop at the edge of the bed, peering down, studying the costume. I glance up, Rosie's eyes already on mine, a twinkle in them.

"That boy really outdid himself this year," she chuckles, shaking her head.

"Why? What did Archer do?" I frown, glance back down, my fingers tracing the edge of the silk.

"Nothing, Grace," she smiles widely, all toothy and white, making my cheeks heat. "Come. Let's get you dressed, shall we."

It's not really a question, she pulls my towel free and hands me a tiny scrap of white lace. I eye it curiously, then draw my gaze back up to hers. I blink at her and this time *her* cheeks heat, even though I'm the one standing here in the nude.

"Where's the rest of it?" I ask and she blushes furiously.

"Well, they're, um, here. Like this," she holds them out to me, and I cock my head.

"They're see-through," I state, unsure why anyone would wear clothes that don't cover them.

I thought that was the whole point.

"They're Brazilian knickers," she says like that explains anything at all.

"What makes them Brazilian?" I ask, stepping into them where she holds them out to me.

"It's just what they're called, Grace."

"But why?"

"Because it's just a popular cut of underwear they wear in Brazil."

I hum in response, even though that doesn't make any sense to me, we don't have English knickers. Well, not that I know of anyway. Rosie lifts the floor length gown from the bed. Holding the white dress up in the air, pinching the skinny straps between her fingers. She helps me manoeuvre into it and then stands me before the mirror, fluffing out the straight skirt and removing imaginary pieces of fluff. I drop my gaze, blinking at the skin peeking through the slits on either side of the long skirt. I run my hands over my chest and tummy. Hard pieces of plastic sit beneath the tight lace fabric of the top.

A boned corset, made entirely of lace, the fabric almost as see-through as my underwear. Thicker material in the cups for my breasts, it pushes them up high and I raise a brow. I'm not sure how I feel about that. The top is tight all the way down until it reaches just above my hips. The fabric turns to silk, long, flowy white silk, a slit up the front on both sides, revealing my legs when I walk. I perch on the edge of the bed, Rosie slipping my feet into pointed flats, white silk also. Everything matching.

"What am I supposed to be?"

Rosie gets me to my feet, making me do a little twirl and then stands me back in front of the mirror. Leaving me to stand here while she goes to fetch something. I shift on my feet, uncomfortable knowing my reflection is *right there*. I take a deep breath, squeeze my eyes shut.

Inhale.

Exhale.

Inhale.

Exhale.

Breathe.

The bedroom door opens at my back, I spin, desperate to keep my gaze from falling to myself.

Thorne stands in the open doorway. A black suit, black tie, black shirt beneath it, a clothing bag in one hand. He cocks his head, his eyes scanning over my body. Not in the same way that Hunter looks at me.

"What are you supposed to be?" I ask him a little louder than usual, he keeps telling me to be more authoritative.

He smirks, the smile on his lips deadly.

"I'm a mafia man," he winks and I'm not sure what that means, but I don't get to ask more questions. "You look simply ethereal, Grace," he tells me, and I know he thinks it's true because Blackwells don't tell lies.

"What am I?" I ask quietly this time, nervously. "I don't know what I'm supposed to be."

"You're an angel," Thorne says as though it were obvious.

I glance down my body, eye my dress. It's beautiful, the most beautiful thing I've ever seen, but I don't know if I've ever seen an angel like this before.

"I have the rest of your costume," Thorne tells me, answering my puzzlement, unzipping the large bag in his hand.

He tugs the zip down and white feathers spill out, desperate to escape the confines of the garment bag. I tilt my head, my brow creasing as he shifts the item out. My mouth pops open, my eyes going straight to his. I blink, lick my lips, take a step closer.

"Wings," I breathe the word, Thorne smiles, watching me approach, my fingers outstretched, they brush over the pearly white feathers. "Will these fit me?" I ask, taking in their incredible length.

The tips of them will surely brush the ground as I walk. Thorne nods, gesturing for me to turn away from him. He threads the straps up each of my arms, tightening them over my shoulders. Adjusting them until they feel comfortable and then steps back.

"Angelic," he states with a nod of his head. "You want to see?" he asks me quietly, his eyes focused on mine.

I shake my head softly, swallowing hard.

"Okay then," he says in that calm manner of his, I've noticed all of my brothers have a certain way with me.

Different to how they speak to Mother.

Mother has openly glared at me every time we've crossed paths since that day in the kitchen. She's steered clear of me for weeks, leaving rooms if I enter, making nasty comments under her breath, not eating at the table for family meals. It makes me nervous. Waiting. Anticipating what horrible thing she's going to do next.

My lungs burn as we reach the stairs, my hand tucked through the crook of Thorne's elbow, his opposite hand clasped over mine. I hold my breath, already overwhelmed by the noise we're descending into, the bottom points of my wings brushing the steps as we walk. We're using the rear staircase, it's not the main one so it's quieter, guests are also not allowed onto the third floor, or into the old mill section of the house. So I'll have places I can hide.

I swallow, my mouth so dry my tongue sticks to the roof of it, I lick my lips, the waxy pale pink coating them only making me drier. I pinch Thorne's arm, he looks down at me as we reach the bottom, turning me to face him. I stare at the two open buttons on his chest, his olive complexion decorated with black swirls beneath his shirt. I continue holding my breath, my lungs screaming as the noise of too many people makes me cringe inside.

"Grace, one of us will be with you all night," he's already promised me this, twice on the way down here alone. "Trust me, Hunter isn't going to leave your side looking like that." He smiles, tips my chin up, presses a kiss to my forehead. "You're perfectly safe inside these old walls, sweetheart, let's go find our brothers."

I finally pull in a breath, my lungs on fire, my chest

rising and falling rapidly. My heart thuds, dull in my ears as I swallow. Thorne links our arms, leading me through the hall, the noise growing louder and louder and it takes everything in me not to cover my ears. My fingers twitch at my side, my light feather wings feeling like they weigh a hundred pounds as we enter a huge ballroom I haven't seen open before.

Every inch of the space is decorated. More glowing pumpkins, white paper ghosts hanging from the gold chandelier, black cats and grey rats cover almost every surface. Fluffy silver cobwebs are strung across the ceiling, the spiders large in an array of bright colours. The polished wood floor is shined, people already dancing on it. Others stand around the edges, drinking and talking, lots of people in varied costumes, all so overwhelming I can't really make any of them out.

Everything is dark though and I feel a little better being in the shadows, until we step through the sliding doors, already pulled open and hidden away inside the walls. A hush seems to fall over the crowd, people slow their dancing, drinks paused halfway to mouths. My lashes flutter, I try to swallow again and almost choke. Thorne doesn't seem to notice, or maybe he's just used to the attention he's currently getting. He has an important job and is the eldest in the family, so it's no wonder people stare at him as we enter. I see Wolf, hiding in the far corner and I desperately want to make my way there, but instead, Thorne leads me towards a long table on the far side of the room. Platters of small foods and strangely coloured bowls of drink cover the top, my eyes scan everything as we pass it. I frown, unsure where it is we're heading when I see him.

His tall, lean body stacked with muscle, half in the shadows, half in the light. My tummy clenches, my heart fluttering like a bird in a cage. I forget there's anyone else in the room as Thorne unlinks our arms. Hunter takes a step toward me and my breath catches. He towers over me, dressed head to toe in black. Fitted black slacks, a black shirt, the top two buttons open, long sleeves folded over, up to his elbows, revealing his strong forearms. A black belt and shined black shoes, his ebony hair styled over one eye. The other eye is wide and dark, swirling with honey caramel, as it drops to my feet. His gaze slowly making its way up my body, he licks his lips, bites the edge of his bottom one. But it's his costume accessory that has me closing the distance between us. My fingers reaching out, the inside of my wrist brushing past his shoulder. I stroke the soft feathers of his black wings. Wings which match mine.

"What are you?" I whisper in the dark between us, the lights dimmed further, Thorne absent at my back.

Hunter steps into me, the noise of everything around me disappearing completely. One hand going to my waist, his grip firm, the back of his other hand running down my upper arm. His knuckles grazing over my skin, goosebumps flaring to life in his wake. I shiver as his fingers link through mine, pulling me into him. I crane my neck, looking up into his eyes, he dips down, lips against my ear.

"The Devil," he whispers.

His tongue licking up the side of my throat, I lean into him, his big hand on my waist tightening. He breathes against the wet trail he created, my teeth chattering. He groans in my ear almost silently, his chest rising and falling rapidly. I feel his chest brush against mine as he pulls me in, eradicating any small distance between us.

"And you're the angel I'm going to destroy," he breathes the words against my cheek almost silently.

I groan, my eyes rolling into the back of my head as his hand caresses its way up my arm. He discretely sweeps the pad of his thumb over my erect nipple, he's subtle enough that anyone looking our way wouldn't be able to see what he's doing. He takes a step back, taking me with him, drowning us in the shadows. It's where we're safe, in the darkness. I feel the wetness between my legs, the throbbing in my lower belly, the burning heat rushing through my veins. He presses himself against me, his long, thick cock already straining against his pants, hard and wanting. Ready to do filthy, rotten things to me, and *God*, I want him to.

"*Mmm,* you look good enough to eat, little sister," he rasps, his teeth against my hammering pulse.

He nips my skin, pinches my nipple, squeezes my waist. I gasp, rising up on my tiptoes, pressing myself closer. He plants his hand on my chest, thick fingers splaying over my racing heart.

"Tell me, Gracie," he hushes in the air between us, brings his face level with mine. "Will you let me devour you, baby girl?"

I breathe hard, my lips almost brushing against his but not quite, I lick them, the tip of my tongue catching his top lip. I nod slowly, my eyes locked on his. He twirls a strand of my curled hair, his gaze dropping to where he pinches it between his thumb and finger.

"Use that pretty voice, beautiful girl," he instructs, a whispered order, my legs almost buckling beneath the weight of the look he gives me.

I drop my gaze, inhale, look up through my lashes, eyes flicking between his.

"I want you to consume every single piece of me, Hunter," I confess, safe in the shadows with this dangerous boy.

His lips crash into mine, his mouth parting instantly, his tongue forcing its way between my teeth. He drags me in, my chest to his, my back arching. His other hand cups my cheek, his thumb on my bottom lip, he pulls it down over my teeth, fingers putting pressure on my jaw. Fucking my mouth with his tongue. He tears himself away from me too quickly, leaving me gasping, a small smirk on his swollen lips.

"Dance with me," it isn't a question.

"I don't know how," I say quietly

Hunter takes my hand, curling our fingers together, he turns me to face the room, and I can *feel* eyes on us as we emerge from the safety of the shadows. My skin crawls like it's covered in insects with too many legs. Suddenly the sound in the room comes crashing back into me and I wince. Too loud, too loud, too loud. I shrink back, colliding with Hunter's chest. His strong arms loop around me, both hands on my belly, he keeps me tight to his front, my large wings crushed between us.

"*Shh*, baby girl, I've got you," he whispers into my ear, my heart pounding. "Close your eyes, listen to my voice." I do as he says, letting myself fall into him, wishing I could crawl inside of him, let him keep me safe forever. "I want to dance with you, beautiful girl, show you off to every-fucking-one."

He spins me around, my eyes closed tight, his hands finding the small of my back, he drags me into him. Using one of his hands he guides my own, placing my palms onto his solid chest. He resettles his hand on my back, his hot skin sending warmth through my cold flesh.

Music is playing, something slow. I tune out the words that sound like someone's had their heart broken and focus entirely on Hunter. He pulls my head against his chest, my hands curling around his waist, fingers curling into the back of his shirt, beneath his black wings. He moves us back and forth, and I feel like I'm floating, like my feet aren't even touching the ground. The songs change, the beats faster, but we don't change our pace, and I don't hear it. I only hear Hunter.

His whispers into my hair, his warm breath fanning across my face. His scent in my nose, the forest after rain, the brook, fresh daisies, earthy moss. I forget where I am, who's around, I lose all conscious thought of everything but him. This beautiful, dangerous man, who keeps me safe and teaches me to read. Hunter is *soft* with me, I've realised. Even in every brutal move he makes, he cares.

He protects me.

I let myself drift into a different place, Hunter's possessive grip grounding. His fingers press into my skin so hard I know I'll have bruises, but it makes me feel seen.

Wanted.

Desired.

Real.

Hunter draws back from me, his hands sliding to my ribs, his thumbs pressing in. He looks down at me, smooths my hair back from my face, watches me for a moment.

"Come, little sister, I want to show you something."

CHAPTER 16
GRACE

Hunter takes my hand firmly, his easily double the size of mine. I remember the first time he held my hand like this. In the dark, the rain, I was lost in the middle of the forest until he found me. He knew my name; I didn't know his. He swaddled me in his shadow, his scent invading my nose, his warm touch, despite the cold rain, comforting on my skin.

We walk through the hallway, decorated with orange and purple streamers, thrown over every light fixture, picture frame and statue. Cauldrons filled with sweets and flickering candles fading away inside Jack O'Lanterns. We take the back corridor, the one that leads to a wide wooden door, steep steps behind it. We take our time heading down, Hunter unlocking his bedroom door once we reach the bottom. Swapping hands with me so he can use the big iron key, and not have to let me go. I like that.

He pulls the door open wide, stepping back and

guiding me through ahead of him. He turns and relocks the door, placing the key on a hook beside it. I greet Tyson and Duke warmly, my palms outstretched. They both stick their cold, wet noses into my hands, licking my skin. I push them away gently, both of them jumping up into the leather armchair, curling into one another, a fur blanket tossed over the back of it.

I turn back to Hunter, standing in the doorway, his hands in his pockets, his head cocked, thick black hair hanging over one eye. We stare across the space at one another. Neither one of us speaking. I swallow, my hands clasping together in front of me, bony fingers knotting. I drop my gaze when it gets too much, too intense. Hunter's eyes scorching me like a blue flame. Too much and not enough all at once. I stare down my body, encased in delicate white fabrics, slits showing my almost equally white skin. I squeeze my hands together, fisting them, my knuckles desperate to pop but unable to as I continue to squeeze.

Hunter is suddenly before me, one of his big hands over mine. He gently applies pressure to my hands, silently urging me to stop. I comply. Loosening my hold, he takes my hands, one at a time, massaging the flesh back to life. Silence between us that I can normally read, but now is fuzzy and unclear, like a veil has been dropped between us. It makes my chest ache, and my heart clench and tingles race up my spine with unease.

"I want to show you something, Grace," Hunter finally says, and I force my gaze up to his, my eyes flicking beneath my lashes. "I don't want you to be afraid, baby girl. You're so, *so* brave, I know you can handle this." He looks up at me, tilting his head in the opposite direction, dipping his chin, trying to claim my attention. "Do you trust me?"

I peer up at him, my eyes wide, something at the back of them pricking.

"Yes," I whisper the forbidden confession.

He smiles that Hunter smile and I melt. It's small, half-hidden, almost just a smirk, but it sparks something in his dark eyes. Something that excites both him and me. He steps forward, kissing my lips so softly I can't be sure I've felt it at all and then he spins me. He turns me sharply towards the door at the far end of the room. The one he often stares at but doesn't open. I glance up at him over my shoulder, my brow creasing. We come to a stop, he reaches around me, a key in his hand, iron like the one for his bedroom. He pushes it in the lock, turns the handle, his other arm banded around my chest, keeping me as close as he can whilst we both wear obnoxiously large, feathered wings.

He pushes the door open, walks us forward into the dark, closing the door softly behind us. The room is so cold I shiver instantly. I blink, fluttering my lashes, trying to adjust them to the darkness when I lose his touch. A cold draft suddenly fills the space where he had been pressed against me. I strain my ears, buzzing inside my head, I can't hear anything over my own increasing breaths.

"Hunter?" I call out into the dark, my voice trembling, I fist my hands.

The space around me is too much, the shadows suddenly unsafe without him by my side. A click, a flash of bright light. I frown, my eyes squinting against the sudden splash of light eradicating the darkness. I look up, towards the sound I heard. Hunter hovers his hand over a light switch, his eyes wide, alert, not even attempting to adjust to the sudden brightness. My eyes remain locked on his, he cocks his head, his hair falling further across one eye. The other an endless pit of black. I open my mouth, close my mouth.

I follow his line of sight at his silent instruction, his gaze slowly moving across the room. I take it all in now, the floor and walls are stone, the same stone as is on the outside of the huge house. Strip bulbs across the ceiling, a table on one side full of instruments. There're no windows in this room, an extractor fan, like the one in my bathroom. A covered table sits in the centre. I take a step closer, an odd shape beneath the sheet. I glance up, my chin dipped, eyes on Hunter. He nods, encouraging me closer, he remains at the far side of the room, his hand resting on the wall now, placed beside the light switch. I move up to the table, every step closer slowing. A tremor wracks through my body, my teeth chattering, I bite the inside of my cheek. It feels like winter in this room, like the room at my school beside the walk-in freezer they used to lock us in without any clothes when we broke the rules.

I uncurl my fingers, shaking out my hand at my side. My hand reaching for the sheet, I glance back to Hunter. His shadow is huge against the pale stone wall, one hand tucked into his slack's pocket. Half of him in shadows cast by his huge black wings, only serving to make him even more beautiful. My fingers dance across the sheet, a thick white cotton, my eyes remaining on Hunter's, I pull the sheet back.

I don't look down, I don't breathe because I think I know what I'm going to find. I think I've known what sinister thing was hidden behind the wooden door I never wanted to open, all along. I think of Hunter's hands, how he scrubs them clean, a mixture of water and bleach. He told me he worked for his family, among others. *Disposals*, Stryder said. I finally, *finally*, suck in a breath, my lungs burning. I look down, release the sheet, it floats to the floor, landing just over my left foot.

A man, grey skin, light hair, lies on the metal table, a drain at one end, the table slightly tilted. He's naked but I don't look, I can't take my eyes off of his face, a perfect hole in the centre of his forehead. There's no blood. No bruising. The skin is parted around the hole perfectly. I tremble, my skin so cold I feel frozen. My hand is outstretched and I'm not sure when I raised my arm. I watch as though I'm not me, as though I'm floating up above, looking down. Watching this dangerous boy hiding in the shadows corrupt the strange girl with the wrong eyes. And I think I like it. I want to be consumed by Hunter; I want him to devour every last piece of me until nothing is left.

My voice is strong but quiet, and I've spoken before I really know if I want the answer or not. Nothing this beautiful dark boy tells me is going to make me feel any differently. I don't want it to.

"Do you kill them, Hunter?"

My finger hovers above the hole in the man's head.

"Sometimes," he rasps, his deep voice echoing around the large, cold space.

I touch my finger to the opening, no bigger than a copper penny, but that's rather large for being in your forehead.

"And when you don't?"

I dip the tip of my finger into the cavity, press it inside, up to the first knuckle. I can feel Hunter's eyes on me, burning into me.

"They get sent to me."

So simple, so normal, so *nothing*.

"Do you care, Hunter?"

I feel nothing either, as I force my finger deeper, to the second knuckle, wriggle it around a little.

"No."

I tilt my head to the right, the side of my face brushing against my white feathered wings. Angel wings. *Because I'm good.* I thrust my finger inside the hole, as far as I can.

"Do you care about anything, Hunter?"

And I'm suddenly holding my breath, the tip of my index finger pressed inside a dead man's skull and I'm not really thinking about that at all. My lungs ache, heavy and full. I lick my lips.

Waiting.

Wishing I was better.

Wishing I really was *good*.

"*You.*"

My legs almost buckle, my free hand grips the edge of the table, I lean my weight on it as I catch myself. In seconds both my arms are pulled back, my body spun around, the icy table digging into my lower back, my wings crushed flat against it. Hunter stares down at me, his chest heaving, his big hands on me, one on my hip, the other on my jaw. He clamps my teeth into my cheeks, their sharp little points carving into my flesh as he applies more and more pressure to my face, my lips popping open.

"Don't *ever* touch another man. Dead or alive, don't fucking do it, Gracie."

I stare up at him, holding his gaze, I don't blink. My hands relaxed at my sides, I slowly raise one, bring it to my face. Pop my finger between my already parted lips, the one that was just *touching* that other man, swirl my tongue around it. Hunter rips his hand from my face, his hands going to the underside of my thighs. He heaves me up, slamming my arse down on the table beside the body. I gasp as he smacks his hands down either side of me, the entire table vibrating beneath me. I arch myself forward, my bum touching the man behind me, my oversized wings catching on his bare flesh. Hunter leans in, dips his chin, looks up at me with dark eyes from beneath those heavenly thick lashes.

He comes in closer, his face in my neck, he runs his nose up the side of my throat. Inhaling deeply against my skin. His tongue in my ear, he bites the lobe, nibbles his way up, licks down the side of my face.

"You're a sick fuck, little sister," he whispers, cool breath blowing against the wet trail he left across my skin.

I shiver, arch into him, he bites down my jaw, nips at my chin. My hand comes up, fists in his hair, dragging him nearer, his lips finding my chest. We will *never* be close enough. Having his touch, his scent, his tongue all over me will never ever be enough. I just need more. I'll always need more. He brings his face to mine, breathing hard, his lips hovering over mine. I lick my lips, my tongue catching on his parted ones.

"You're a sick fuck too, *big brother*," I whisper the words over his lips and then his mouth is on mine.

His teeth clash with mine, a shockwave vibrating through my skull. He kisses me, his tongue licking into my mouth, caressing my own. His lips suck and pull, his tongue teasing mine. I fall into him, my fingers fisting the roots of his hair. He growls into my mouth, his big hand roughly parting my legs. He steps between them, yanking me closer, forcing the back of me into the body.

"Hunter," I gasp, trying to break our kiss as he nips at my lips.

"Mm?" he hums, his teeth and lips frantically climbing down my throat, his big hands everywhere all at once and I can't think straight.

"I-" his hands slide between the slits in my dress, exposing my legs.

"You…?" he palms my thighs, fingers edging the lace of my knickers. "Tell me what you need, baby girl."

Breathing hard, I pull back, look into his eyes, deep chocolate brown, flecks of gold. I bring my hand from his hair, trace his jaw, smooth my thumb across his cheek. My touch soft, gentle, soothing the monster that lies inside of him.

"You. Just you," I breathe in the small space between us.

He lets his eyes fall closed, my hand clasping his face, his warmth seeping into my cool skin. He exhales, like he hasn't been able to in a long time. His head on me, resting against my collarbone. I comb my fingers through his silky, black hair. Hold him to me, his big hands squeezing my thighs, he glides them up, settling on my waist. His hold on me something I never want to lose. I feel so much in his presence that I don't know how to feel anything at all.

He draws back, his perfect plump lips parted, his breaths deep and even. That sharp jaw, square and masculine, his straight nose, the jagged scar through his eyebrow.

"Grace, I-"

I slap him across the face.

His head snaps to the side, his eyes roll open as he turns back to face me, swirling pools of warm chocolate turning midnight black. His grip tightens on my waist, his thick fingers flexing over my protruding rib bones.

I breathe hard, watching his face. His eyes narrow, I lick my lips, bite into the bottom one. He nods to himself, a sadistic curve to his lips. He releases me, steps back, leaving me sitting on the table with a corpse. I slump back a little, using the body to prop me up. I hear Hunter across the room, but I don't turn, even as I hear him clanging metal, shifting things around. I close my eyes, let my head fall back, facing the ceiling, I swing my legs gently. The soft fabric of my dress swishing around my legs. I feel Hunter before I hear or see him. I keep my head back, neck exposed to a predator, his scent filling my nostrils. I want to reach out, grab hold of his shirt, curl my fingers into it, tear it from his body. But instead, I sit, patiently, knowing he's going to have his hands back on me soon.

I'm his addiction as much as he is mine.

"You want to play, baby girl?" he whispers against my ear.

I shudder, a smile curving my lips, I hum in response, biting the inside of my lip.

"You look fucking beautiful, Gracie," he rasps, his teeth plucking the skin over my pulse point.

I imagine his teeth sinking beneath my flesh, his teeth clamping down on it, his jaw locking, ripping the pulsing artery free from my throat. My heart pounds as his hand slides over my breasts, his fingers splayed, palm stopping over my heart.

Does he know it only beats for him?

"What will you do," he says quietly, hairs stand to attention all over my body, "when I rip this out of your chest?" he whispers, his other hand twirling a strand of my hair between his fingers.

I don't open my eyes, I keep my head back, my long blonde hair likely draping over the corpse on the table behind me. I hear a soft snick, something metal, and I keep my eyes closed. I don't want to see it; whatever it is he has. *I don't want to see.*

"Get off of the table, baby girl."

He hefts me up, gently places my feet down onto the ground, turns me in his hold. My back to his front, his arms band around me, his hips pressing me against the table. My lower belly warm on the inside from his touch, cold on the outside from the icy room, the cold metal table against the thin fabric of my dress. His hands run down my arms, his thick fingers coming over the backs of my hands, lacing through mine, his palms on the backs of my hands. He holds something in his right hand, pressing it between our joint fingers.

"Keep your eyes closed," his voice smoothing over my trembling body, he can feel me shaking, he ignores it.

I lay my head back against his chest, his arm with the object going forward. I flinch as my fingers touch the man; I try to pull away. Conflict inside my head.

Don't ever touch another man. Dead or alive, don't fucking do it, Gracie.

"This time it's okay," Hunter whispers, his deep voice coiling around me like a constricting snake as he answers my silent question.

Always knowing.

Always there.

Always inside my head.

"You and I, we belong in the dark. We're safest in

the shadows, baby girl."

His lips make their way up my neck, his teeth scraping up the column of my throat. The feathers from our wings tickling against the back of my neck, my bare shoulder.

"Keep those beautiful eyes closed for me and just feel, Gracie. Just feel. Trust me."

I do as he says, letting his hands move mine, touching cold skin, tough beneath my fingers. I shrink back into him, his grip tightening, my knuckles clicking beneath his hold, but he doesn't let go.

Never let me go.

Hunter presses our joint hands down onto the man's chest, our fingers feeling our way over his chest cavity. I shiver, tucking myself back against Hunter's warm chest. Our other hands, the metal object wrapped in our intertwined fingers. He angles us, our wrists pointed down, the object pressing beside the fingers of our other hands. I suck in a sharp breath, my eyes squeezing tight as we pierce into this body. Cool liquid covers my fingers, cover his, sticky and thick, as he guides me across the man's torso, pressing harder in some places over others. I breathe hard, my eyes still shut tight, I lose track of time, Hunter's muscular body against mine. His cock hard as steel beneath his slacks, twitching as he presses it into the small of my back.

"That's only for you, no one else could ever make me this fucking hard, little sister," he breathes against my neck.

His chin resting on my shoulder, our hands still

carving into the body.

"You look so fucking beautiful coated in blood, baby girl."

He kisses my shoulder, his words comforting the darkest parts of my soul. The parts that have always been there, pulled out meticulously by his. Drawn from the deepest depths to dance in the shallows. I would be nothing if it weren't for Hunter. I didn't even exist in the real world before. And now, now I'm living in it.

I'm alive.

Even when he makes me want to die.

For him.

With him.

My heart beats so hard I don't know how it hasn't torn free from my chest, ripped its way through my skeleton and offered itself up to him in sacrifice.

My stranger.

The Devil.

My Hunter.

I relax into him now, my body going lax, my muscles like liquid, as calm as the lake we swam in. I breathe in, smelling iron, smelling the forest. Moss, daisies, the babbling brooks. I sigh, the deepest, longest exhale. My bones go numb, my head feels light, and a smile curves my lips. I stay that way, letting Hunter use my hands for his work. Knowing I'll never say no to this man. Not that he'd let me, anyway. But I'll die before I give him up. Everything he is, I am, *we* are, fills me up and I laugh. The softest huff of breath. Hunter stops what he's doing, we release the metal tool.

"Open your eyes," he breathes against me, making me shudder.

Slowly, I blink my eyes open, my lids heavy, the room bright. I look down, blinking softly, the man's skin cut away, sliced delicately, crafted like a tapestry. Hunter steps around me, nudging me back a small step, he uses a small silver saw to cut down the centre of the man's chest.

I peer around him, watching as he places the saw to one side, forces his hands between the man's ribs. His thick fingers working their way into the centre of his chest. I can't look away, fascinated as he uses his entire body to flex his grip, fingers curling beneath bone. Finally, he grunts, sweat glistening on the back of his neck, black wings swaying gently. He parts the two pieces, a sickening crack resounding in the air.

"You want this, Gracie?" he coos over his shoulder, ushering me closer.

I step up behind him, looking at someone's insides.

My fingers reach in, featherlight touch to his heart. I look up, my hand still inside the cool body. Hunter's eyes full of life, a sparkle, as bright as the sun in his gaze. I nod softly.

I step back, giving him room, swallowing hard as he reaches in with both hands, curls them around the heart and savagely tears it free. The organ dark and lifeless, he cups it in his big palms, turning towards me, his eyes immediately on mine. The ghost of a smile on his beautiful face.

"For you, little sister," he murmurs, dropping the

heart into my open hands with a small thud. "I'll bring you whatever you want, a thousand hearts, eyeballs to entrails, whatever your heart desires, I'll get it all for you," he whispers between us.

Stepping into me, I look up at him. My heart pounding, my tummy churning, my thighs clenching with need. Wetness floods down the insides of my thighs, slick and ready. Wanting him to destroy me in every way he sees fit, whatever he wants to do to me, for the rest of my life, I'll let him. Welcome it, whatever it is. I just want him. I stare at his handsome face, his straight, black hair hiding one eye. His black feathered wings still firmly in place, despite our demonic activities.

An angel I suddenly realise.

My angel.

My safety in the shadows.

The angel of death.

I drop the lifeless organ to the floor, my hands going straight for his face. I grab him, pulling him down to me in a hurried kiss. My tongue sinking into his mouth, his hands run down my body, gathering my skirt at the hip, he tears it up one side, the silk and lace cracking as it rips upwards, stopping just beneath my breast. He hoists me up, my arse hitting the cold table, my thighs thrust apart. His tongue attacking mine, our mouths, teeth and lips mauling one another as he hurries to free himself from his slacks. My hand finds his cock, palming his thick, silky length. He tears my knickers to one side, the lace cutting into my upper thigh, his teeth tearing into my lip. I line him up with my entrance, our movements rushed, hurried, everything moving pace at a million miles an hour, he thrusts inside of me.

"I love you," he whispers over my mouth, his words against my lips.

I flick my gaze up, my heart stuttering to a stop inside my chest. I gasp for breath, his thumb on my bottom lip, bloodied fingers fanned across my cheek. I swallow, the tang of blood, from the body, from me, from him. *Us.*

Silently, his hands go to my thighs, gripping my flesh, he pulls me into him every time he thrusts inside of me. My core tightening with need, my pussy desperately trying to suck him deeper. I bite into the side of his neck, tearing at the buttons of his shirt. They bounce and ping across the floor as I rip his shirt open. My greedy fingers curling over his solid shoulders, nails carving their way beneath his flesh.

He fucks me relentlessly, our mouths collide, teeth tearing pieces out of each other as he slams his dick deeper and deeper inside of me. I tighten around him, feeling every single inch of him as he hammers his dick into my cervix. My walls flutter around him, desperate to accommodate his thick cock. His hands on my thighs spreading me wider, his fingers digging into the hollow space at the back of my knees. I grind myself against him, my clit hitting the hard packed muscles in his lower abdomen every time he thrusts back inside. He draws almost all the way out of me, before forcing his huge cock back inside me. Over and over and over again.

"Hit me," I grit out, breaking our kiss.

His forehead finding mine, he breathes me in, his nostrils flaring. He reaches around me, his other hand still on my thigh. He lifts something up, holds it beside my face.

"I'm not going to hit you, Gracie," he tells me through gritted teeth, his cock still sliding in and out of me, his pace slowing.

He draws back, a sliver of space between our faces. I glance left, a blood-stained scalpel between his fingers. I lean back, arch my neck, expose my throat.

I don't want to be saved.

Make me hurt.

Every time he looks at me, my heart flutters, my tummy flips, my entire body thrums with adrenaline. Hunter makes me feel. I don't want to ever leave his side, but I will gladly die by this man's strong hands if he deems it so.

I don't close my eyes, I stare into his, making sure those beautiful chocolate orbs are the last thing I see.

This strange forbidden love always had to come to an end.

"What are you doing?" he frowns, stilling inside of me completely.

I stare at him, cocking my head, blinking.

"What?"

"I'm not slitting your throat, Grace," Hunter growls, his knuckles blanching around the small blade, he stares at me a long, long moment and then a darkness falls over him. "What the *fuck*?" he bellows, pulling himself out of me completely.

His expression turning into twisted fury. I grasp the edges of the table to keep myself from falling to the floor. He fists his hair, pacing the room, mumbling under his breath. I sit quietly, wondering what I did wrong. My chest hurts, my curled fist going to the centre of my breasts, pressing into the bone and rubbing. I look down, twist my hands in my lap, hands and thighs streaked in crimson. Heat pricks the back of my eyes.

"I don't understand," I whisper to myself.

A strangled sound gets caught in my throat, my chest heaving as everything inside me churns. But then he speaks, and I think everything's going to be okay.

"You want me to hurt you, Gracie?" he asks from somewhere behind me, his deep voice low and threatening. "Is that what you want, beautiful girl? You want me to hurt you?"

My lip trembles, chin wobbling and everything inside of me cools to a degree below freezing.

"I can hurt you, baby girl. I can bury you if you want, you'll be such a pretty corpse. Lying naked upon my table, where a thousand other *insignificant* bodies have lain before, waiting for my blade."

My head snaps up at that, his words cutting me bone deep. He scoffs a laugh, that twisted smirk on his face. He cocks his head, wandering back towards me, my skin prickling with goosebumps as he nears. I grasp my torn skirt, cover myself with it, then he's there and his hands are on mine and he's tearing it away.

"Nu-uh, let me see what's mine," his voice soft, teasing, his eyes as black as the night's sky.

He comes before me, tears my thighs open, even as I try to keep them together. Pressing himself against my core, I can feel how hard he is still, his dick twitching as it meets my heat. I fight back a groan, push at his chest, fight to keep him away, but he grabs my hands in one of his, holds them brutally behind my back, twisting my arms, shoulder sockets popping.

It hurts and I like it and I wish I didn't.

But he knows.

He *knows* that I do.

Hunter knows everything about me.

Every thought, feeling and sick little want running through my skull. It's why we play this game. I hurt him; he hurts me back. I try to push him further; he ends the game early. But I don't think that's what's going to happen tonight. I don't think even Hunter could stop this right now if he wanted to. So I'll play along. I'll fight back and enjoy the hurt. Even if it kills me.

"I love you," he whispers again, my chest tightening. "I don't need to hear you say it, baby girl," he reassures me, *knowing*. "It's okay, because I know, okay? I fucking know," he breathes, his warm breath against my lips.

My eyes fall closed at his gentle tone, the truth, in his words, I feel it, and something *else*. Something uncomfortable rushing through me, it fuels my excitement.

"You think I'd kill you?" he whispers the question, his deep voice smooth and slow, lips brushing mine.

I open my mouth, attempt to answer, but I just don't know what to say, so I close my mouth, swallow instead. Keep my stinging eyes closed.

"Tonight," he rasps, his voice sending a shiver down my spine. "I'll absolve your sins, you'll absolve mine," he feathers the words against the shell of my ear.

He hums, his tongue lapping at an escaped tear sliding down my cheek.

"You're so, *so* fucking beautiful when you cry, baby girl."

He suddenly releases my hands, his fist knotting in my hair, tearing my head back. I gasp as his fingers pinch into my thigh, the scalpel nicking my skin, beading with blood. He doesn't care, doesn't stop, I clamp my legs together which only serves to drag him in closer. He smirks down at me and slams his way home.

I cry out as the head of his cock hits my cervix, strangled sobs leaving my throat as he fucks me brutally. My hands fly to his throat, my fingers squeezing his neck. He laughs, a deep, throaty chuckle filling the echoey room. I dig my nails in, my fingers turning white as I apply my entire body weight behind my hold. Hunter rips my head back, long golden strands snapping free from my scalp. I slap him, and I can feel his cock getting even harder.

"Do it," I hiss, my lip curled. "*Cut. Me.*"

The air crackles around us, his dark eyes flicking between mine. His thrusts punishing as he slams his cock inside of me. I'm getting wetter and wetter and it's audible now, I can hear it, he can hear it, that wet slapping, and he smiles. He smiles so broadly that I try to inch back, but his grip is too tight, and his eyes are almost black, pupils blown. He truly is the Devil.

"If you insist," he spins the blade, slices it into my left thigh and carves lengthways, stopping just before my knee, he throws the blade to the floor.

Blood blooms, bubbling up through the cut, oozing its way out of the neat line. I watch it spill over, run down the side of my thigh, soaking into my white dress beneath as Hunter continues to fuck me. So when his thick fingers find the wound, pressing and squeezing, pain tearing through my soul, I explode. I come, coating him in my release, gripping and milking his cock as it continues to hammer away inside of me. I cry out so loud I could wake the dead man behind me if he still had all of his insides. Hunter bites down on the crook of my neck, his big hands gripping and pulling me into him so tightly it crushes my bones, stealing my breath. He groans, filling me with his release. His hot cum painting my insides, my walls fluttering around him as his dick pulses.

Unknotting his fingers, Hunter smooths down my hair, pulling me into him. He kisses my temple, once, twice, three times. His lips melding to mine, he kisses me, tears fall from my eyes, and we bleed together. Drowning in whatever it is we've created here, an addiction, something dark and unusual. I kiss him like I need him to survive. And he kisses me back the same way. Neither one of us wanting to exist in a world where the other doesn't.

So we'll keep playing these dangerous games, until it really is the death of us.

CHAPTER 17
GRACE

I arch my back, my spine clicking as I stretch my body out along the mattress. I can smell Hunter beside me, feel his heat, hear his even breaths. I reach out, my eyes still closed, my fingers wrapping around his bicep. I sigh, curl myself into his side. His thick arm comes around me, tucking me into his muscular body, his grip crushing. I blink my eyes open, looking up at him, his dark chocolate eyes already on mine, the rising sun casting him in warm light.

"Hunter," I whisper, letting my eyes fall closed again.

"Grace, I need to talk to you about something," his deep rumble vibrating the words through my bones.

"Mmm," I sigh, snuggling in closer, wriggling my toes, my eyes pop open. "Where's-"

"I put them outside a little while ago," Hunter interrupts, answering my unspoken question about the Dobermans.

I look up at him, sling my arm over his waist.

"Why?"

Ignoring my question, Hunter sits up, my arm falling away, he twists away from me, giving me his back. I sit up on my haunches, my hands on my knees as Hunter stands from the bed, pulling on his tight-fitting joggers. Seeing my nail marks slashed into the tops of his shoulder blades, I reach down, finding the long slice in my thigh. I smile softly as he turns to me, frowning when he sees where my hand is. He dips down, grabbing some loose tartan pyjama pants from the floor and throws them my way. I stand from the bed, following his silent instruction and pull them on. Sweep my hands down my thighs, little, short dog hairs dusting them.

"I can't do this anymore, Grace," Hunter says coldly.

I glance up, his eyes on mine, his expression blank.

"Do what?" I blink up at him, the bed between us.

His hand running through his hair, he shoves it back, away from his face, both eyes visible.

"This, us, whatever the fuck it is we're doing here, it has to end."

"End?" I echo, my lips parted, the breath sails out of my lungs, and I think I might faint.

"I don't want to be with you anymore."

My chest aches as I look over at him, studying his face, my tummy dips and I feel like I'm being hung upside down. Everything is the wrong way up, bile rises in the back of my throat.

"I think it'd be best if we stayed out of each other's

way for a while," he says casually, pushing his hands into his pockets.

Stay out of his way.

"Dad can hire you a tutor to help you with your reading and writing, and for anything else you might want to learn, just let him know what you need, and he'll sort it out for you."

Wake up. Wake up. Wake up.

I press a fist to my lower belly, grind my knuckles into my skin, take in a shuddery breath.

"Just make sure if you go out into the woods, you take someone with you, or the dogs. I don't want to be sent out there to find you again."

Sent.

Everything is spinning, the world is tilting and I'm falling. My breath rushing in and out of me, my chest heaving and burning. My brain is on fire, my lungs are screaming but I'm not actually doing anything at all.

I stand stock still, my breaths slow, my heart thudding evenly. Hunter stares at me and I drop my gaze. My cheeks heat and I wonder what I'm doing in here. What did I ever think I was doing here? I don't fit. I thought everything was wrong but it's not, it's just me. *I'm* wrong. I shift on my feet, my body flushing with uncomfortable heat as I feel his eyes boring into me. His eyes setting my skin ablaze, as his words flay my insides, burning me up until I'm nothing but ash. I want him to take it back, tell me he's lying.

Blackwells don't tell lies.

I thought that was something good, something

admirable. But now I think it's possibly the worst thing I've ever heard.

"I'll have Rosie bring up any of your things."

I hold out my hand, palm outstretched, I'll do just about anything to get him to stop talking right now. I lick my lips, and I can taste him, and it makes me want to throw up. His scent in the room suddenly so overwhelming I want my lungs to shrivel up and die like the rest of me.

"But you said, you told me that you loved me," I whisper, blinking back tears.

I look up at him, heavy silence hanging between us, he looks at me like he's never seen me before and my oesophagus closes in on itself, my windpipe crushing every word. Wishing that he really had cut me up into little pieces last night, after all, instead of filling my head with his sick, sick poison.

"Yeah, well, I lied," He sighs like this whole conversation is boring, an inconvenience he wishes he didn't have to deal with.

My chest caves in, my heart finally slowing to an almost stop.

"Blackwells don't tell lies," I breathe the words out, wishing my traitorous tongue could have kept them in.

"How would you really know that's true when you aren't one. You're a Bishop, your mum just happened to marry my dad, he didn't adopt you, you were never a Blackwell."

My heart sinks into my stomach like a lead brick. The phrase that made me feel like a part of something when I first arrived here, made me feel a tiny glow of warmth inside my chest when I was all by myself, stolen away from me and burnt to ash. I press my hand to my heart and step around the bed, move past Hunter towards the door. My silent tears hit the floor as I go but I don't draw attention to them. I just want to get out of this room before I lose myself completely. The door's already unlocked when I pull it towards me, something that never happens, meaning he'd been waiting for me to wake up just so he could throw me out.

I don't know how I find my way back to my bedroom, or when I run a bath and get in it, hoping it will drown me. But when the room falls dark and the water goes cold, and the sponge I used to scrub my body down with is stained red. I crawl my way out of the bathroom and prop my aching body up against the large window. My eyes focused on the swaying trees, the wind howling, it whistles through the dark room, and I let my eyes fall closed. Praying that I wake up and this was all a bad dream.

Three days.

Three days since I closed the door, locked it and flushed the key.

I stare out across the woods. Rain has been falling since I locked myself away. Day and night without letting up. The trees dancing to an unheard melody of melancholy. The wind howls through my room, a chill creeping over my already cold skin. I rest my head against the freezing glass, let my teeth chatter. My hair hangs down my back in knots, my face unwashed. I squeeze my fingers in the fabric of my hoodie. Pulling the sleeve up to my nose, I breathe *him* in. Hunter's scent starting to fade from the pull over hoodie and tight joggers that I rescued from my clothes hamper. The material drowns me in every way but I'm still cold.

I stare out over the grounds, rain lashing against my window. I've been watching. Waiting for Hunter to make his way back on Lady, my eyes are so heavy they feel like they're sinking into my skull, but I can't let them close. I can't do anything until I see him again. I cup my sleeve covered hand over my face, covering my nose and mouth. My eyes still locked on the woods. There're no birds, no deer, rabbits, foxes or squirrels. It seems they disappeared about the same time I did.

I wonder if I'll die in this room, how long it will take anyone to find me. No one else uses this floor. Just me. In the furthest corner of the house. Tucked far, far away. Hidden from sight, easily forgotten. Rosie tapped at my door this morning. I didn't move. She rattled the handle and then I heard her sigh. And I haven't moved since. I don't know if I'm even breathing unless I can smell him. Tears fill my eyes, welling up, spilling over my bottom lashes. I don't blink them away, I just stare out, desperate to catch a glimpse of him. He's probably avoiding this part of the house; it's been a long time since I watched him gallop away. It was still dark, the sun trying to rise, blocked out by the heavy rain clouds.

Sometime later, I'm still sitting in the dark, curled against the window. The glow from the stables far off in the distance holds my gaze, even as the wind whips branches across the small beam of light, I don't lose sight of it. My face still wet, I sniff, wipe my cheeks against the sleeves of my hoodie. The glass making a permanent indent in my temple where I remain pressed against it.

I try to breathe in, my ribs feeling like they're curling into my lungs. I push my hand down my jogging bottoms, fingers finding the long slice in my thigh, it's healing, scabbed over, dry. I pick at it, still staring out of the window, my fingers digging and scratching at the cut. The glass like ice beneath my cold cheek, I pull my hands inside my sleeves. Curl my fingers into the thick fabric, bring them to my face. Daisies, moss, something metallic.

"*Gracie.*"

My eyes snap open at the sound of his voice, head smacking into the window. I blink into the dark room. Shadows from the trees outside dancing across the walls like ghouls. I slow my breathing, my racing heart hammering in my chest. I squint into the darkness. Movement across the room catches my attention. The door to the hall wide open. I lick my lips, trying to see, when the bathroom light switches on.

"Get up off the floor, Grace," Mother snaps, the light blinding me as she heads into the ensuite.

I hear cupboard doors opening and closing, shuffling as she goes through the things beneath the sink. She hurries back into the room, her slim figure dressed impeccably as always. A form-fitting navy pencil skirt, cream blouse tucked into it. Her pin heels clack across my wooden floor, her hands going to her narrow hips as she stops before me. I stare at her feet, my gaze safely away from hers.

"Get up," she commands, her foot tapping against the floor.

I uncurl my body, my legs screaming as I wobble to my feet. My head spins, my hand slapping against the window as a wave of dizziness crashes over me. My tummy cramps, my mouth so dry I can hardly swallow. Pins and needles race through my tight limbs, arms and legs, feet and hands, nothing ready to function after being locked up tight, unused for days.

"You look awful," Mother clucks her tongue, "hurry up and put your shoes on."

She turns away from me, kicking a pair of canvas pumps in my general direction. I wriggle my feet into them, my toes uncooperative as she waits by the open door, huffing, arms folded over her chest. I make my way over to her, little white spots splattering my vision. I blink hard, my eyelids heavy, hefting my loose jogging bottoms up higher. Holding one side of them over my hip, they might be tight-fitting on *him*, but they swamp me completely. I follow Mother silently down the hall, then the stairs. I move as quickly as I can as she hurries me out of the front door. The icy rain hits my skin, pelting me like little stones falling from the sky.

"Get in," she snaps, her tone brittle.

I climb inside the waiting car, clipping my seatbelt into place. She slides into the seat beside me doing the same. The car pulls away as soon as she tugs her door closed and my heart pounds hard in my chest. I glance out the window, the giant stone mansion dark inside its windows. I look back over my shoulder as we drive down the driveway.

"Where are we going?" I ask, my tongue heavy in my dry mouth, flicking my gaze out the side window, trees rushing by.

I catch sight of my reflection, and I can't look away. I stare at myself, deep dark circles beneath my bloodshot eyes. My hair a wild mess, my mouth tugged down in a sad frown. Tears instantly prick my tired eyes.

Mother scoffs, "*we* are not going anywhere, Grace."

My belly flip-flops, my teeth tearing into my bottom lip at the way she accentuates *we*. My fingers flex, my eyes lock on the door handle. The car is zooming down the road, trees rushing past my pounding head in a flurry of darkness. I raise my fingers, latch onto the handle and pull. Nothing.

"What were you going to do, Grace, throw yourself out of the moving car?" Mother chuckles in her seat beside me. "Why do you think you're here with me?" she asks me, happiness in her tone, I don't get to answer. "The Blackwells don't want you there anymore. You stupid, stupid little girl. Couldn't get my husband to fuck you so you thought you'd go after his weirdo son instead," she harrumphs. "Didn't work out so well for you, after all, did it?" she laughs lightly, the sound making my skin crawl. "I've found you a nice new place, now that you're all grown up, you'll be with people more like *you*," I see her shudder in the reflection of my window, the outside of it streaked with rain.

She reaches inside her bag, perched in the footwell between her feet. Pulls out a few boxes, their foil packages rustling inside.

"Now, be a good girl and take your pills."

CHAPTER 18
HUNTER

This house is a tomb. Quiet, cold, dead. Just like the inside of my aching fucking chest. A boned coffin for the deceased organ.

I wish it would fucking kill me.

Four long fucking days have passed. Today is the start of day five. The fifth day since I shredded her heart, ripped it out, spat on it, set it on fucking fire. She hasn't left her room.

I can't feel her today.

I've sat alone in this basement bedroom, listening to this lifeless house creak and echo around me and I swear I could feel her. I could feel her pain as real as my own silently calling to me. Begging me to go to her. Wrap her up in my arms, fingers knotting in her golden hair. My lips smothering hers, pulling the breath from her lungs. So many times, in the last hundred sleepless hours, I've had to force myself to remain down here. Keep my distance. Make myself bleed instead of her for a change.

I can't feel her today.

I can't smell her in my sheets, or on my unwashed skin. I can't feel her breathing when I place my hand against the old stone walls, residual energy that was all *her* locked up inside. The only evidence of her I have left is her blood smeared across my bottom bedsheet. Deep red staining the white sheet. Blood. From her thigh. The wound I carved into the surface of her skin. Always fucking hurting her. I hate myself. I gave her the fucking control. That day in the lake.

I hit her back.

I scrub my hands down my face. My stomach growling with hunger, my head dizzy with lack of sleep, mouth dry with only sips of water. I forgot how to function without her. I rub the heels of my hands into my closed eyes, pressing until I see stars behind my eyelids. I thought I was doing the right thing. For her. For me. But all I've done is destroy her. Like I intended. And myself in the fucking process. I never thought I'd fall in love.

I can't feel her today and I want to die.

I called Arrow.

My little brother.

The *sweet* one.

He's coming home today. To see her. For me. I told him what I did. Why I did it. I told him things I've never told anyone before. About me. About her. *Us.*

He didn't understand it.

The violence.

But he understood the hurt. Pain is a universal language.

I push myself to stand, my legs feeling like a newborn deer as I stagger into the bathroom. Stripping my joggers, twisting on the taps I force myself into the shower. The spray like ice pellets against my back. My hands splay over the jade marble wall, my head hanging forward between my hunched shoulders. I squeeze my eyes shut, the water still like ice, my eyes grow hotter, I hold my breath, reaching out to her inside my head. Praying to Satan something will force us back together.

What I did.

Why I did it.

I thought this was all to keep her safe.

From me.

Herself.

I thought I'd taken it all too far. I don't want to wind up killing her. The way she bared her throat to me, waiting so willingly for me to take her life. If I ever accidently hurt her enough to- I can't think about it. I'd die without her, for her, with her. I separated myself from her to keep her fucking safe.

I got scared.

She scared me.

I scared my fucking self.

I did this all to save her.

I screw my eyes shut tighter, my insides hollowed out, hot tears stinging my cheeks like acid as they fall. More punishment, my penance. For ruining this beautifully broken girl. A fragile treasure snapped between my brutal fingers. Something that smelt like innocence but tasted like sin. Looks like an angel but carries a piece of hell inside those bones. Her eyes, one crafted by the Devil, the other blessed by God. Perfect. She's fucking perfect.

Perfect for me.

My fingertips curl into the wall, muscles cording with tension. I heave in a deep breath, my heart thudding so slowly I don't know how I'm still standing. I'm ready to die. I have nothing without her. I *am* nothing without her. We'll be each other's undoing.

I'm trying to save her.

I don't know how to breathe without her. A beautiful fucking destruction. All of her was made specifically for me. I'll never have anyone else. I'll never want anyone else. And I'll kill anyone who tries to touch her.

Stay away. Stay away. Stay away.

I grab the soap, wash my body, shampoo my hair, scrub my skin. Anything to make me leave her alone. Keep me at a distance. I need to eat, to leave this fucking room. I need to fucking breathe, get outside, check the horses, run with the dogs. But I can't force myself to care enough to do any of those things.

I can't feel her today.

I want her. I want to hurt and fight and fuck. I want to sink my fucking teeth into that perfectly translucent skin, drink her blood, slather it all over her perfect body. Have her do the same to me. Drink me down, fill her veins with me. Never even think of letting me go.

I let her go.

I set out to destroy her. I thought it would give me something to do. I thought I'd enjoy it. She got under my skin. Those huge fucking eyes, mismatched and unblinking. Staring at me in wonder, marvelling at what they saw when she ran her curious gaze over me. My body, every inch of my face. Her small hand in mine, bony fingers laced through my thick ones. How I could crush every bone in her fucking hand, and she'd still want me to hold her.

We are the creeps in the darkness. Skulking through the shadows. Together. Forever in the dark. I never want us to leave, never venture out into the sun. I want us to drown in the safety it offers us, the veil of comfort it provides. We can do anything together in the dark. We were made for it, *of it*. The two of us just need to feel and bleed and fight and fuck and laugh and cry. And feast off of each other. Destroy one another. And then pick up all of the fractured pieces, put each other back together. Retreat back to where we live. Together.

In the dark. In the dark. In the dark.

I grit my teeth, turn off the water, throw a towel over my body. I grab clean joggers off the armchair. My body still sopping wet, hair dripping water down my face. It rolls down my nose, drips to the floor as I tug on my bottoms, the fabric clinging to my wet skin. Forgoing everything else, I take the stairs two at a time, burst out of the door, it smacks into the wall, bouncing off, ricocheting, slamming itself shut. I rush down the hallway, my feet slapping against the wood, water pouring off of me, a trail of wet footprints in my wake. I take the next set of stairs, the main ones. I move through the upper floor, head towards Grace's bedroom.

I don't know what I'm doing. We're going to kill each other but I wouldn't want it any other fucking way. I just need her, and I can't stop myself. Because if I'm going to die, it might as well be with her. For her. By her fucking hand. Not sulking alone in the belly of this stone beast we call a home. Not when she's just two floors above me.

Give in.

I grasp the brass handle, press it down, force the door open. I rush inside, my eyes darting all around, the bed made, the window seat empty. The spot in the corner she likes to sit against the glass, bare. The bed made, room neat. I push into the ensuite, empty.

I can't feel her today.

I fist my hair, panic like fire rife in my veins. I rush out of the room, pound my feet back down the stairs, slip in the water I left behind but keep going. Rush towards the kitchen, hearing deep voices.

"Where is she?" I boom, my usually quiet voice bouncing off of every wall in the kitchen as I enter the open archway.

Dad's place at the head of the table empty. Arrow, Archer, Raine, all three surrounding his empty seat. Two oldest on the left, youngest on the right. All three sets of eyes on me. My chest heaves as I try and fail to get myself under control. Lungs rapidly trying to draw in breath. I slam my hands down on top of the table, thick plastic tablecloth beneath my palms. I rock forward, my fingers splayed.

I can't feel her today and I know something's wrong.

"Well?" I growl, low, threatening.

Arrow's endless pits of black bore into me, a pitying expression on his face. I hiss through my teeth; I don't need anyone looking at me like that.

"Dad and the boys have gone after them," Raine says calmly, like *that* means any-fucking-thing.

I turn my gaze on my youngest brother, my eyes narrowing. I bite the inside of my cheek, sniff, close my eyes, exhale.

"Someone better start fucking talking, right now, or I am going to lose my fucking shit."

I breathe in, oxygen burning my throat as I rapidly pull it into my lungs. My fingertips dig into the table, elbows locked as I hunch forward. Stare down my brothers.

"Eleanor-" Archer starts, but I don't need to hear another word because I already fucking know.

I already fucking know.

I'm fucking coming for you, baby girl.

"Hunter!" Arrow shouts as I spin on my feet. "She's not worth it," pleading in his voice, he doesn't want me to regret it. "Dad will sort it, the boys will sort it. Wolf and Thorne, they'll get her back. We just have to wait a little while longer. And then, *then* you can sort her. Think this through, man. That's Dad's wife."

I feel him move, shifting out of his chair, stopping just behind me. My chest heaves, my fingers curling into fists, clenching, knuckles popping. I grind my teeth, nails digging into my palms. My nostrils flare, and I can prac-tically taste his hesitation in the air when he lays a hand over my shoulder. His fingers squeezing. I let my eyes close, my back to my brothers so they can't see pain twist my features. Fury razing its way across my flesh. I suck in a sharp breath, like stabbing in my lungs. A knife pushed between my rib bones, corkscrewing its way inside my chest cavity.

"Where is she?" I ask, just needing the confirmation, deep down I already know.

The options are slim, it's not easy to hide someone if you do it properly, but this is the new Mrs Blackwell. And she might be a slimy little cunt but she's just not that fucking clever. I have no doubt Dad got the address out of her in under three minutes, but I need to know because I need to go. I need to be there.

And as insane as it is, I don't want my brothers' fucking hands on her. Regardless of the situation, that girl may be their sister now, but she's *my* fucking girl, and I'll break their goddamn fingers.

"St Michael's." It's Archer's voice this time, the *happy* one, the joker, the fuckboy.

But you couldn't guess that from his tone; dry, cold, angry. Laced with an emotion I can't quite read, but one I think I fucking like.

He gets Wolf on the phone, telling him we're on our way. I don't hear anything else. My own thoughts swirling around inside my head, making it impossible for me to listen to him. How did she get her out? When? How long has my Grace been locked inside a cult run, mental institute for the damned? They better pray to their so-called Gods on their hands and fucking knees that they haven't had a chance to touch a single golden hair on her pretty little head yet. Because if I get there and they have, they will wish they had never been born. No one touches what's mine without paying for it in blood.

And Grace.

Grace is mine.

So when Raine pipes up behind me, his lighter wheel flicking, the flame hissing, over and over and over.

And he says, "let's burn it fucking down."

I smile.

CHAPTER 19
GRACE

"**K**eep still."

One, two, three, four.

"*Swallow your pills.*"

One, two, three, four.

"*Take your hand out of your trousers.*"

One, two, three, four.

"*Stop or I'll break your fingers.*"

One, two, three, four.

"*Crazy fucking bitch.*"

One, two, three, four.

"*Get her in a jacket.*"

One, two, three, four.

"*She bit me!*"

One, two, three, four.

"*Put her in the cell.*"

One, two, three, four.

"*I'll get you back for that.*"

Everything is cold. My legs are bare, my teeth are

chattering, and I can't think. My brain is aching, my head heavy and big and everything is loud. I try to clamp my hands over my ears, but I can't, my arms locked over my chest, bound in thick, scratchy fabric. Like my old clothes. From my old school.

School.

I squeeze my eyes shut tight. My head against the mattress covered wall. Everything in this spongey room is too bright. Everything is white and it makes me want to claw my eyeballs out of their sockets just to give them a break. But I can't do that either. I can't do anything with my hands.

Hunter. Hunter. Hunter.

I exhale, the pain in my chest almost as bad as the fire in my fingertips, but I ignore both. Bring my leg back up towards my chest, force myself to strain forward again, hunching my shoulders. My mouth finding my knee, my eyes still closed, I feel along the cut with my lips. My tongue sliding over the torn skin, tasting copper and salt. I bite into my new wound, the one Hunter carved into me. It wasn't deep, it was a shallow cut just meant to bleed. But I need this wound sliced down the length of my thigh to remember. I don't ever want to let him go.

It is real.

He was real.

It wasn't just a dream.

Tearing and chewing at the cut, I wipe my face across my thigh, spit little slivers of skin to the floor. I bite and chew along it, making sure it doesn't fade, ripping it back open. I need it so that I'll know. Even though he doesn't want me, and it makes me want to die, I'll always know I had him.

Hunter.

I keep seeing his face, hearing his voice, and I swear I can feel his touch on my skin. I know it's inside my head, but I keep letting myself go, wander with him when he reaches down and takes my hand, suddenly unbound. I'm sick but I know he was real.

"You're a crazy fucking bitch."

My head swims and my arms scream with pins and needles. I take a break, blood running down my leg, my neck cracking as I straighten a little. Lying against the wall in the far corner of the too big room with too much white and everything is soft. And the smell isn't right and there're no bars on the windows because I haven't got one.

I smack my head against the wall, repeatedly slamming my face into it, made of fucking fabric. I need it to hurt. I've got nothing without the hurt.

I scream. Hunter's voice shutting me up.

"You want me to hurt you, Gracie?"

I scream and I scream and I scream. Until my voice is hoarse and my mouth is dry and tastes of blood as I bite the inside of my cheek. I gag, swallow the bile rising in my throat.

"Is that what you want, beautiful girl? You want me to hurt you?"

A sob chokes me, my lungs squeezing painfully. Tears stream down my face. I lick my lips, salty and wet, a copper tang I won't ever get rid of. I headbutt the wall. Praying for it to suddenly turn to concrete so I can smash myself into it until I never have to wake up. I'm not strong. Not since I've been outside, I gave my heart to a beautiful, dangerous boy who crushed it beneath his boot. He made the hurt so good I don't know what to do. How to think, how to breathe. Everything inside of me aches. I try to curl my fingers. The ones without nails. And my hand burns, pain racing up my forearm, elbow, all the way to my shoulder until it's a screaming pain in my temples.

I smack my face into my knee, hard, and then I do it again. My head spins, my body feels like it's falling through the air, light as a feather and then I hit the floor, heavy, like I'm made of lead. The ground beneath me still soft but my head hurts, my ears ring and I feel the first few moments of relief. I stop forcing my eyes to stay closed, they just stay that way as I clamber back up onto my bum, knees drawn up to my chest, bound arms trapped between. I balance in the corner, side of my body propped up against the wall, back to the door where people come to gawk at me. I suck in a long, slow breath, and throw my head into my knee.

I hit the floor before I feel anything, side of my face pressed into the mattress. I let my eyelids flutter and I swear I hear my angel roar.

Hunter.

I sway like I'm in water, the gentle tide lapping at my skin. I think of the lake, of Hunter's hand colliding with my cheek and warmth starts to work its way through my icy veins. Something hot, trickles over my brow, down into my opposite eye. And I think I've struck gold because I know it's blood. My forehead thuds, my pulse echoing around my skull, my heartbeat so loud in my ears, it feels like someone's crashing cymbals together inside my head.

I let go.

I let everything go.

My body weightless.

My mind fuzzy and clouded like a stormy day.

I feel his hands then, smoothing down my bicep, the same hand sweeping hair back from my face. I feel it unstick, from my bloody skin, be pushed carefully behind my ear. I breathe in and want to smile, and I also want to die. The brook, that fresh scent of water, lightly perfumed daisies and rich, heavy moss. A shadow falls across my face, my eyes still shut but the inside of my eyelids are no longer a bright orange, now they're a muted pink, and it feels better. The dark. I relax then, my body melting into the floor, thick fingers tracing my jaw. Another hand on my back, the tinkling of buckles, and my arms start to drop a little. My eyes open slowly, I blink against the harsh light, but it's easier now, with the shadow over my face.

I'm lying on my side when my jacket is untied, the buckles and thick straps being loosened, pulled open. Hands gently moving me to my back, the shadow still covering me, I peer through my lashes, my eyes so heavy.

Hunter's dark eyes stare down at me, his face just

above mine. His thick black hair, sharp, square jaw, and dark full lips. His hand on my cheek, thick fingers so gentle, I press into his touch. Let my eyes fall closed again, pray that this is it.

Maybe this is it, and wherever it is I'm going to after this life, whoever is taking me, they gave me this one last thing. They let my beautiful, broken boy with the black wings and the dangerous smile take me there.

I'm lifted then, up into his arms. My angel clutching me to his firm body. I press my ear to his chest, his heart hammering so hard I feel its vibrations crash through my jaw. But I don't care, I press myself against him harder, trying to crawl inside his chest cavity and let him absorb me into his soul. Meld us together instead of letting me go.

He already let you go.

None of this is real.

A sob gets caught in my chest, choking off my air supply and I slam my head against his chest. All hard muscle and thick bone, it hurts, pain rushing through my face, high pitched ringing inside my head. I do it again, sobbing into his shirt. My brain rattling around inside my skull, I finally go still, let my body go heavy and pray this is death.

I'm shifted around, my head over his shoulder, legs wound around his waist. A hand on the back of my skull, an arm propped beneath my bum, I cling onto him, as he holds me like a child. Sobs slowing even as my tears continue to fall, soaking into his shirt. I clutch at the thin cotton, one hand curling beneath the round neck, the other gripping at his shoulder. I cry out, my fingertips on fire, pain hurtling through my bones, I grit my teeth, hold my breath.

"Shh, Gracie, I've got you."

The Devil coos. A trickster. He can make you see things you wish were true, hear them, feel them, nothing but blood laced sacrifice demanded in return. I open my eyes, eyelids heavy, and see a long hallway, all white tiles and bright bulbs. My head lolls into Hunter's neck, my lips against his skin, I peer over his shoulder as he takes me wherever it is we're going.

That's when I start to see them.

Bodies.

Bent necks, twisted limbs, and blood. So. Much. Blood. It's splattered up the walls, trailing across the floor, like something was dragged through the puddles of mess. I tilt my head, my vision still obscured by my lashes. A man, hanging from a ceiling fixture, prisoner jacket like my own over his head, buckled up tight around his face. He swings in place, blood covering his white coat and pale green outfit. And it makes me smile. As my angel carries me further away, six more familiar faces start to follow behind us. Each one with dark eyes and darker hair. An arrowhead formation follows behind us and I finally let my heavy eyes close.

I grit my teeth as I'm pulled back against a soft body, I arch forward, trying to get away, not wanting to touch anyone. My trousers ripped from my legs, cold fingers pinching at my flesh. A long slice down my thigh, all the way to the knee. I want to keep picking at it, clawing, scratching, but they take my hands, pulling my arms at odd angles. Two men, one woman. I've never seen any of them before.

I don't know how I got here.

The two men have my arms, my fingers desperately trying to claw at them, they slap at my hands, bending back my fingers until my elbows ache and I think they might break them. The woman steps closer, now that the person I'm being held by has twisted my legs between theirs. I can't kick out at her as she approaches. Her light eyes have a sinister glint to them, blue handled pliers in her hand. Before I know what I'm doing, I spit in her face. She snarls, her lip curling, swiping the back of her hand down her cheek.

"You'll pay for that, you little bitch," she hisses at me, venom on her tongue, spittle flying from her mouth.

Wake up.

The man holding my left hand forcibly uncurls my fingers, bends them back, then laces his sweaty hand through mine. Bile rushes up my throat, my stomach convulsing, but I haven't really eaten this week and it's making my insides full of pills churn with acid. I struggle in their hold, try to wrestle my arms away.

You're dreaming.

"If you can't stop picking at your goddamn leg, then

we'll make it so you can't pick or scratch at anything at all. We'll do this every fucking time until you learn your lesson."

I don't know who says that, I don't know anything, my fingers are on fire. Tugging and pulling and red-hot pain spreading through my hand like it's been doused in petrol and a match has been dropped. I'm panting, I'm sweating, and I'm so dizzy I don't know which way is up and which way is down.

I bolt up, gasping for breath, my hand going to my throat. My eyes ping open, glancing around so fast my head whirls. I heave in breath after breath, sweat on my brow. My other hand fisting the sheet pulled over my legs, soft cotton. I tilt my head, looking down, white linen with pale blue daisies, shifting my gaze up, I look out of the huge window that takes up one wall in my bedroom. The autumn sun just drifting below the trees.

Wake up.

I push the sheet down, past my knees, little white, silk shorts hitting the tops of my thighs. The large wound on my thigh covered with a thin bandage, not the thick scratchy kind. Kicking my legs over the side of the bed, I press my hand to the bedside table, steadying myself, a glass of water, handful of pills.

You're dreaming.

Pushing to my feet, I glance down, little silk camisole loose on my bony body, my chest exposed, arms too. My fingers on my left hand stiff, a dull ache rolling through them, the tips in delicate bandages. I cock my head to the other side, heading towards my door, listening to the house creak around me. It breathes, this house. It's walls made of old stone, so much energy trapped inside it, laughter and love and pain. The hurt fuels the rest, it flexes, it gives, and it absorbs.

Absolves.

I'll absolve your sins, you'll absolve mine.

My dark angel dropped me here for a reason.

I curl my fingers around the brass handle, push it down, silently step into the hall. I can practically feel *her*. In this house, this beautifully haunted house, there is a rot. A black source of decay. I'm going to excavate it from this place. Take it with me when I journey to hell. Let it burn forever.

Wake up.

I take the back staircase, keep to the shadows, the house is silent as I sweep my way down the hall to her bedroom. The one furthest away from mine. I can smell her perfume, sickly and sweet, my nose wrinkles. I stop before the double doors, hands hovering just over the handles when I hear her. Humming to herself, *happy*.

Mother.

You're dreaming.

Happy.

Because I'm finally gone, again. I ruined her life and she threw me away at six years old. Picked me back up at eighteen, reluctantly, under order, for her husband. I mean nothing. To anyone. I did for one short fleeting moment. I meant something to *him*. Even if only for a short time, it was real. Tears prick my eyes. I swallow down the pain in my chest, force the shuddering breath out slowly, calm myself. Then I press down on the handles, step into the room, silently close the doors at my back. A haze of perfume and hairspray fill the air, the vile mixture threatening to choke me. I clamp my lips between my teeth.

Wake up.

This room is large, a suite of sorts, a large mahogany desk on one side, a sofa and armchair on the other, open suitcases spread out over the floor. Light colours decorate the space, creams and beige, a soft carpet beneath my bare feet. Two doors on the back wall, I assume one is for the bathroom, the other the bedroom. One door is cracked open, Mother's humming coming from inside. I tilt my head, wander towards it. I sweep my fingers along the top of the polished desk as I pass it, stopping just before it as the humming stops.

You're dreaming.

The door opens, Mother stops in the opening. I don't look away.

"Grace! What on earth are you doing in here?" her shrill voice snaps in surprise making me wince, but I keep my eyes on hers.

Staring into them, a soft hazel, flecks of green, gold, so much like mine, less sad, more lifeless.

"What happened to you?" I ask quietly, my voice dry, I lick my lips.

"What?" she snaps back, "stop looking at me, for Christ's sake."

She hurries around me, leaving as much space between us as she can. I drop my gaze then, down to the desk, my back to her now. A pot filled with pens, a marble coaster, message pad. My fingers dance across the little bowl of paperclips, a sheet of red postage stamps, a gold letter opener, in the shape of a little sword. The handle engraved with an intricate pattern.

Wake up.

I take it between my fingers, a hefty weight in my hand for such an insignificant object. I hold its handle, cool in my clammy palm, finger the long blade with my bandaged fingers. Press the point into my palm, close my hand around it.

"I asked, what happened to you?" I repeat my question, my voice calm.

Because I'm strange, delicate, too soft, like a dandelion, destroyed by nothing more than a small breeze.

"I was wondering who hurt you to make you this way," I offer my explanation gently.

You're dreaming.

"You have got some nerve, little girl," she growls at my back, her voice low and gravelly, full of rage.

I understand that.

"You're upset with my question," I observe, my back still to her.

Wake up.

"I'm not *upset* with your question," she hisses. "I'm furious with it! I am none of your business, you nosy little bitch!"

I nod gently.

"Now, get out of my room, you shouldn't be

wandering around this house, young lady and you know it."

"Was it your mother?" I ask, turning towards her, spinning the gold letter opener in my hands.

Her hands balled into fists at her sides, a vein pulsing in her temple. Pale blonde hair in perfect curls at her shoulders. A silky cream blouse, top button open, tucked into a navy pencil skirt, gold chain around her neck, pearls in her ears.

"Get out."

A small smile twitches at my lips.

"It was."

You're dreaming.

"Get out!" she screams, her hand flying in the direction of the door, finger with pale pink polish pointing towards the wood.

I take a small step forward, in the direction of the doors, *her* direction.

"If your mother was as nasty to you as you are to me, it makes me wonder why you're the same. Why do you do the things she did if it hurt you so much?" I keep my gaze on the little gold sword in my hands.

"I should have cut you the fuck out of me when I found out I was pregnant with you. Your daddy was evil too, that's where you get it from, it's not in *my* fucking genetics. All of this strange fucked up behaviour!" she yells now, but I don't look up, I can't.

Wake up.

"It's nothing to do with me, you're the spawn of Satan himself, you were *forced* inside of me. I never wanted you! I was cursed with you. And now you've ruined my life again! *I* have to leave. Let me tell you something, *Grace*," she hisses, getting in my face now, I keep my eyes averted even as she points a perfectly manicured finger in my face. "You are nothing but a disease, one I should have cut out. An infection. You disgust me. I wished every day I was pregnant with you that I would miscarry. And then when you were born, with those strange fucking eyes and blank fucking expressions. I wished every fucking day you would just *die*."

Wake up.

I smack my hands against the front of her shoulders, knocking into her so hard she stumbles back, her arse hitting the floor. She scrambles backwards on her hands and feet, trying to get away from me. I stalk her across the room, taking my time, my bare feet sinking into the soft carpet. I climb on top of her, pin her arms over her head with my bandaged fingers, straddle her waist. My heart is banging against my ribcage, desperately trying to tear free from its boned bindings. My chest heaves, she thrusts up, trying to dislodge me. My brain hurts, my eyes watering.

"You silly little girl, what are you going to do? Huh? You think they won't lock you back up when they find out you assaulted me? Your own mother," she scoffs. "You're so fucking dumb, weird, unhinged, deranged," she spits the words in my face, my eyes closing. She laughs, it's sick and my insides churn. "You are *nothing*. They'll throw you away too, just like everyone always will, Grace, because you mean NOTHING!" she roars in my face as I bury my little blade into her chest.

Wake up.

My entire weight behind it, I tear the gold sword out, slam it back in, beside the first wound. She coughs, blood on her lips, splattering across my face. I release her hands, put both on the warm metal and plunge it into her, tear it out. Over and over and over. I'm panting, sweat running down my back, I stab her until I can hardly lift my arms. I slump against her slick body.

"Why couldn't you love me?" I whisper against her bloodied face, burying my face in the crook of her neck.

Wake up. Wake up. Wake up.

CHAPTER 20

HUNTER

"I'm sorry about Eleanor," I sigh, scrubbing a hand down my face.

And I am, I mean it. I just want my dad to be happy, but he has terrible taste in women. Eleanor's a cunt. Currently upstairs packing her fucking bags. There's nothing Dad loves more than his kids. His first wife, my *mother*, found out just how much, after she sent me away, Dad came and got me. I was thirteen, it was the longest three days of my life. We never saw her again. We like it that way. Thorne has the most issues when it comes to her. It wasn't just me she hurt. Each of us have issues and it all boils down to that woman. So the fact there's a second woman in our lives abusing her kid? He'll never stand for it.

Dad'll go after her and dispose of her properly. He's just making her think she's safe. She doesn't know what we do, but she knows we're dangerous. She doesn't care, she was only after Dad's money, after all. He told her to leave, wrote her a cheque, she said she'd go pack. It'd almost be funny if it weren't for everything else going on.

He claps a hand down on my shoulder, long, thick fingers curling into my flesh, he squeezes me tight, and I feel my muscles uncoiling.

"It's okay, son," he smiles at me, that Dad smile that tells you he's fine, but you know deep down he isn't.

I don't know what he ever saw in Eleanor, but it still makes me hurt for him.

Grace is upstairs, passed out in bed. The amount of drugs in her system enough to tranquilise an elephant, she'll likely be out a couple more days. I've never been so uncontrollably angry in my entire life. When we got to that backwards, cult-run monstrosity they call a *church for the sick*, I fucked up. I made a mess. The woman that pulled my girl's fucking fingernails out had it the worst. I did the same to her then made her choke on them. Every. Single. One. I've never smiled so goddamn wide. My brothers are out cleaning up said mess. They did help make it, after all, even Dad let out some of his rage. Everything inside of me broke last night, pieces that I just don't think can be put back together.

I think back to just a few weeks ago, being sent out in the dark to find my missing sister. I was pissed off, it was raining and I had a body on the slab. The room's temperature controlled but I like to get on with my jobs as soon as they arrive. And the Swallows have *really* been keeping me busy lately. They're a family like ours; full of fucking psychos.

My mind wanders back to my Grace. My *heart*. Something I thought never had the capacity to love. It doesn't matter that she didn't say it back. I know she does. It's just she's never had anyone love her before. And our love is different. It's dark, it's twisted, toxic. It's everything it shouldn't be, but I wouldn't change anything about it. I can play this game, I can make her see, prove to her how much I love her. I've already killed for her, and I know she'll think that's more romantic than a bouquet of fucking roses. We're complicated and wrong and I want to keep it that way.

I was never interested in anyone, not until her.

A beautiful butterfly I want to pluck the wings from, but once caught between my thick fingers I find they're dipped in poison. They singe my skin like drops of acid, burning my outsides just like she does my insides. I want to catch fire in her gaze, take her hand and let us both burn.

My chest aches, my throat tight, I curl my hands into fists, flex my stiff fingers. Try hard to stay in my seat instead of finding Eleanor and suffocating her in her suitcase. I slump in my wooden chair, pulled out from the dining table, Dad at the head of it, me on his right.

"I didn't mean to fall in love with her," I confess quietly, not much more than a whisper. "She's just- I'm sorry, Dad," I glance up, look over at him.

His deep, dark eyes already on mine, shining beneath thick lashes. He blinks, clears his throat.

"Never apologise to me for that, son. Never apologise to me." He shifts in his seat, hands splayed on the tabletop, he pushes himself to stand, groaning as he does. "All I've ever wanted is for you to be happy, Hunter. I already love Grace as though she were my own. And if she's it for you, I'm happy too." He straightens, his muscles flexing beneath the sleeves of his shirt. "Just, don't take it too far, Hunter. That girl, precious as she is, is just like you."

With a wink he turns, pushing his hands into his pockets, he leaves the kitchen tossing a *'I'll be back later'* over his shoulder as he heads towards the foyer.

I sigh, drop my forehead to the table, groaning at my aching muscles straining beneath my skin that feels too tight. Everything just feels wrong. I click my neck, try to roll my shoulders, my hand going to my nape, I squeeze hard.

"Hunter?"

My head snaps up at the sound of her quiet voice, like the softest note of music to my ears. My eyes wide, I open my mouth, close my mouth. Trying to find the words. *Any* words. My heart pounds in my chest, my mind trying to unpick what's stood before me, a million thoughts rushing through my head.

"I'm ready now," she rasps, her voice dry, words calm.

"Ready for what, baby girl?" I ask as calmly as I can.

Grace's slim body dripping in blood, smeared across her cheek, her jaw, running down her neck. I try to gauge where it's all coming from, splattered down her bare arms, her white shorts soaked in red. Her silk camisole splattered, heavier in some places than others.

Blood runs down her bare legs, dribbling down her ankles, dripping from her hair.

"Hell."

She cocks her head, says it so simply as though I should already know what it is she's talking about. Blood drips from her chin, spattering the floor beneath her. A steady puddle growing. I lick my lips, try to get control of my wayward thoughts.

God, she's fucking beautiful in red.

"Are you hurt, Gracie?"

She pouts, nods her head, tears gathering in those gorgeous fucking eyes. I take a step towards her, around the table, my eyes locked on hers. I couldn't look away if I wanted to, I'm enthralled by her, completely captivated by my blood-soaked angel.

"Where are you hurting, little sister?" I ask quietly, her hand going to her chest, she rubs her thumb down the centre of her breasts when I spot it.

A letter opener curled inside her fingers.

I take in a deep steadying breath.

"What's wrong with your chest, baby girl?" I quiz her softly, my deep voice a low rumble.

She shivers as I approach, my hand going to her waist, the other along her jaw. I stare down into her eyes, warm hazel, glacial blue. My gaze flicking over her face, assessing her for damage.

"It hurts," she whispers, a tear rolling over her bottom lashes, sliding down her cheek.

I lean in, the flat of my tongue against her cheek, I lap at the tear. Salt and copper filling my mouth.

My lips to her ear, "why does it hurt, Gracie?" I pull her into me, a small gap still between us, I take my time closing the distance. "Tell me."

"Mother," she breathes, a tremor rocking her frail body, a small sob escaping her.

My hand sliding to cup the back of her head, other arm around her waist. I pull her into me, her head against my chest. I breathe her in, my nose buried in her hair, the scent of rust filling my nostrils.

"It's okay, Angel, it's *okay.*"

My breath shudders in my chest as she relaxes into me. Her hands climbing up to rest against my chest, I can feel the letter opener against me, crushed between our bodies. But I don't care. I don't care that she's probably just killed her own mother, I don't care that she could potentially do the same to me. I don't care about anything except her, here, trapped in my arms. I close my eyes, press my lips to the top of her head, pull her closer, crushing her in my arms.

"You left me, and now you're supposed to take me to hell, aren't you?" she whispers between us.

I frown, grip her biceps in my hands, move her a fraction back from me so I can look at her.

"What?" I question, her frown deeper than I've ever seen it, confusion flooding every feature of her beautiful face.

"I'm dead," she whispers.

The way she looks at me like I have all the answers. Can fix everything on this goddamn planet, slays me. My heart hammers, my dick straining in my tight-fitting joggers. The longer I stare at her the harder it gets. I grit my teeth, cock my head.

"Baby girl," I lick my lips, smooth her hair back. "You're not dead."

"What? But I…" she trails off, her whisper raspy, throat dry, she stares off, over my shoulder. "You left me, Hunter," she says, almost as if she's not speaking to me at all. "It feels like…" she glances up at me and my heart fucking breaks. "I have to be dead."

"You're not fucking dead," I can't help but snarl. "You're not fucking dead, Gracie, you're not fucking dead, okay?" I shake her shoulders, she shakes her head, even as her body wobbles in my tight grip.

"How can that be?" she whispers, her voice breaking, tears sliding down her cheeks, carving a trail through the smeared crimson on her pale skin. "How can I know, Hunter? How can I know?" she sobs.

I pull her into me, crushing her against me, her body shaking so hard it's a wonder she isn't seizing. Her arms come up around my back, the bloodied letter opener clattering to the kitchen floor.

"I promise you, little sister, you're very much alive." I grab her hand, press it against my chest, my heart hammering against her palm. "You feel that? That's for you. It's all fucking for you. I'm nothing without you, baby girl. I love you, I'm so sorry. I *did* leave you. I thought I was protecting you from me. I thought I was going to ruin you, and I wanted to, until I didn't, and I was scared. I got fucking scared, Gracie, and I'm sorry. I'm so sorry. Please, believe me. You're alive and I'm alive and I want to spend every fucking second for the rest of my goddamn life with you, Gracie. But I can't do that if you don't believe me. I can't fucking do that, do you hear me?"

She stares up at me, her eyes red, glazed with tears. She bites her lip, and I groan, my dick so fucking hard I can hardly think of anything else.

Rain hammers against the kitchen window, the wind howling, the back door rattling on its hinges. I grab her face, drop mine to hers, press our foreheads together, my hands cupping her cheeks.

"I love you, Gracie."

Her hand cracks across my cheek so hard I momentarily see stars, my head snapping to the side. I grit my teeth, flex my jaw, bring my face back to hers, stare into her mismatched eyes.

"Liar," she breathes against my lips.

I chuckle, loud and low, the vibration rumbling through my chest.

"I'll prove it to you," I whisper over her mouth, a tremor wracking through her body as I sink my teeth into her bottom lip.

She pounds her fists against my chest as I dip her backwards, bending her over my arm, dragging her pelvis flush with mine. Her core already flooded with heat as I force my knee between her legs. Her thighs crushing mine in her grip. She groans into my mouth, I swallow the sound, forcing my tongue between her lips. She momentarily tangles her tongue with mine before she realises what she's doing. She bites down on my tongue, swallowing down the blood she spills. I moan into her savage kiss, my teeth nipping at her tongue, her lips. She pushes against my chest, hands balled in the cotton fabric of my t-shirt, unsure if she wants to force me away or drag me closer. I give her no choice either way, holding her against me with brute force.

"Gracie," I groan into her mouth, my hand on the back of her head.

Thunder rumbles overhead, directly above the house. The lights go out, the power shutting off. I drag my lips from hers, panting, her chest heaving against me. I look out of the window, the sky dark, rain hammering down in sheets. A crack of lightning, the briefest flash of light floods the room before we plunge back into darkness. I drop my face back to hers, skimming my lips across her jaw.

"Hunter," she whispers, my spine tingles, a shiver running through my bones.

I breathe hard, dragging her up with me as I stand, backing her into the table. My palms slamming down on either side of her, boxing her in, chest to chest. I graze my teeth down the column of her throat, her hands still fisting my shirt. She looks at me, still so unsure that it breaks my fucking heart.

I grab her jaw, squeeze her face and she smacks me again. The back of her hand this time, snaps out, catching me across the jaw. I snarl at her, baring my teeth, I shove my black joggers down with the other hand, freeing my dick. It throbs against her belly, she squirms back, I squeeze her face harder, shove her blood slicked shorts down her legs. The silk fabric slapping as it hits the floor, pooling around her ankles. Her pussy bare beneath, I can hardly stop myself from coming at the sheer thought of thrusting inside her.

She pants, her heart hammering against my own. I dip my face, teeth latching onto her top lip, I bite down, *hard*. She whimpers, claws at my throat.

"Say it. Say you want me to ruin you. Tell me you want to hurt. Because you like it. Because I like it. Because it's wrong. And so are we, baby girl. We're both so fucking wrong together I don't ever wanna be fucking right."

I feel her fingers flex, her eyes wide, and even in the dark I can see her, staring up at me like I'm her God, her Devil, something she wants to worship and loathe and love all at once.

Her eyes locked on mine, I shift my hands to the back of her thighs, lift her up, slam her down onto the table, she arches forward, the thick plastic tablecloth cold against her warm skin. I grab her arse cheeks in my hands, drag her to the edge, her legs spread wide. I grip my throbbing cock with one hand, her jaw with the other, staring into her beautiful eyes I slam myself inside of her.

I see it then, in her eyes, as she comes back to me. Like she suddenly snapped back into her body, her fingers grip me, her head pressing against my chest. I clutch her to me, slamming my pulsing length in and out of her, working my way inside her. Her walls quivering around my thick cock, desperately trying to adjust to me being inside of her.

"*Fuckkk,*" I hiss. "You're so wet, little sister," I rasp against her neck, burying my cock deep inside her slick cunt, all the way to the hilt.

She arches her spine, her head dropping back, exposing her throat. I attack her translucent skin, trail my tongue over the green-blue veins visible in her neck. Her pulse hammering against my tongue. I nip at her skin, plucking it with my teeth, kiss down her neck, thrust my dick inside her so hard our hipbones snap together with an audible crack.

She threads her hands behind my head, digs her nailless fingers into the nape of my neck. I slam into her harder, thinking of everything that happened to her in the last forty-eight hours.

Because of me.

"I killed them," I rasp against her cheek, dried blood flaking off against my lips. "I killed everyone who laid their fucking hands on you," I confess. "And I'd do it a-fucking-gain," I growl into her, biting into her cheekbone.

She groans, a long, low whine escaping her throat.

Thunder echoes around the room, the shadows encasing us inside them, locking us up in this moment.

This is where we live.

In the dark.

It's where monsters like us belong.

And I'm more than okay with that, as long as we're together, I don't need anything else.

"Don't ever leave me again," she whispers into my neck, her lips skimming over my pulse. "I love you, Hunter." My heart thuds, battering against my ribcage. "I didn't understand before," she sobs against my skin, her tears hot, scalding my skin.

I thrust harder, claw at her back, clutching her close.

"Don't let anyone else hurt me," she begs, her voice quiet but desperate. "No one but *you*, Hunter. You make the hurt burn," she whispers, her head tipping back, my cock slamming so deep inside of her I swear I can feel her cervix against the swollen head of my cock. "Burn with me, Hunter," she murmurs against my lips, my name falling from her throat amidst a moan of pleasure.

I slam my hips hard, thrusting into her with brutal force. My mouth collides with hers, my lips smothering her own, tongue sinking into her, hers instantly tangling with mine. I make love to her with my mouth, my fingers knotting in her hair, I draw her face into me. Our noses smashing together, tongue, teeth and lips never parting. We're both panting, both ferociously trying to claw our way home inside of the other. Our souls colliding just like the clash of thunder overhead. I thrust into her, over and over and over again until she's singing my name, and I'm gritting my teeth, her name a whispered prayer on my tongue. She explodes around my cock as I come inside of her, filling her up with spurts of thick cum. I drop my face to hers, smother every inch of her blood-soaked skin in kisses, my lips tasting and loving every fucking inch of her beautiful face.

"I love you," I whisper into her. "I love you more

than I could ever explain, Gracie. I fucking love you, baby girl."

She takes a deep breath, trying to gain control of her heaving chest, her eyes boring into my own.

"I love you, Hunter," she tells me softly, and I feel those fractured pieces of my heart start to stitch themselves back together again.

EPILOGUE

GRACE
SEVEN MONTHS LATER

The sun is bright, high in the sky, we're protected from its harsh rays beneath the cover of trees. Shadowing us in safety. The scent of lavender fills my nose, the start of summer and the heavy showers we had throughout the month of April making it bloom across the meadow like waves crashing in the ocean. Light filters through the thick branches above us where we sit. A navy tartan blanket spread out beneath us, Tyson and Duke lounging out in the tall grass, rolling on their backs, their bellies exposed.

I think about my new family. A small smile gracing my lips. A stepdad who loves me. Five overprotective, older brothers, all of whom tell me constantly how much they, too, love me. *Especially* when Hunter's in the room. How he threatens to break their necks every single time. *For me.*

I think about my school. About Matron. How I couldn't ever look at myself in a mirror.

I think about Mother, bone-deep hatred in her eyes, the snarl in her curled lip. Venom on her tongue, the vicious words she spat at me. The blood on her skin, the holes in her chest. I shiver, my spine stiffening at the memory.

"You okay, baby girl?" Hunter's deep voice rolls up through his chest, my back pressed against him, I feel it vibrate through my bones, warmth filling my chest.

Hunter sits behind me, his back to a thick tree, legs spread wide, me sat between them, head against his shoulder. His big hands wrap around me, placed protectively over my round belly. I look up, sighing at the warmth on my face. Breathe *him* in, earthy moss, daisies, the fresh scent of the brook. Let him ground me, keep me safe.

Hunter, my protector.

I close my eyes, turn my face into his neck. I nod against him, my lips pressing into the side of his throat. His big hands flex on my swollen belly, thumbs stroking small circles over my white cotton dress. He breathes in deeply, filling his lungs with me. He does that when he needs to feel grounded too. I'm his light, he said, even though I have darkness too.

"You can tell me, *little sister*," he taunts, one hand sliding up my body, stopping at the hollow of my throat.

I huff out a laugh.

"I was thinking about Mother."

"Ah," he says as though he knew, he likely did, he seems to know everything I'm thinking.

He places a kiss to my temple, his hands tightening on me, comfortingly.

"What if I'm like her?" I whisper, turning my face up to look at him.

His gaze snaps down to mine.

"You will never be like *her*," he hisses, scowling down at me.

I swallow, glance away, the hand on my throat gliding up, firm on my jaw, he turns me back to face him.

"Never, Gracie, you could *never*. I don't want you ever worrying about that, okay?" he says gently, and not for the first time do I fall just a little bit more in love with him.

My hand slides over his, his fingers lacing through mine, the one resting protectively over our son. He kisses my forehead, his lips ghosting over my closed eyelids, my cheeks, my nose, lips, jaw. I giggle as he kisses my lips a final time.

"I love you, Grace," he whispers over my lips, breathing the words into me, imprinting them on my soul.

"I love you, Hunter."

THE END

Afterword

I loved writing this book. I can't even begin to put into words how much. I've always loved writing. I've always loved my characters and their worlds. Building it all up to tear it all down. But this book? This book…

I wrote Grace and Hunter's story in a little over four weeks. What started out as a novella length idea quickly snowballed into a full-length novel. I was obsessed with the pair of them, getting their words out, their thoughts, feelings, the interesting and *strange* ways they felt about things. I didn't sleep much, constantly thinking of them and what they were doing.

I hope you loved this story, their world and Hunter and Grace as much as I did. Despite all of the ways this story isn't romantic or sweet, I also think it kinda is. My heart is full right now, and I hope yours will be too.

I was extremely sad writing their ending. Although, I'm more than sure we'll see them again soon. After all, look how many Blackwells there are left to write about…

Acknowledgments

Thank you so much for reading. I couldn't do this without all of my readers' support. So to my beloved Street team, ARC team, and everyonc in between. Thank you.

Jade - for letting me steal your blah trick! For keeping me sane throughout the ENTIRE writing process of this book. For reading pages and pages all out of context and loving it all regardless. For reassuring me my blurb was good whilst my thumb hovered over the delete button. For loving Hunter and Grace as much as me. I love you. Plain and simple. Also, you're a wall, did you notice? A beautiful bathroom wall…

Markie - for letting me talk this through whilst you cooked barbecue. For encouraging my idea, adding your own and helping it flourish. For loving me even though some of my ideas are 'sick and deranged'. Thank you for loving me harder for it.

Leah - I want to keep you forever. Please, run away with me? For your encouragement, your fucking *passion* for Hunter and Grace and their story. For throwing yourself so completely into this last minute project and making the entire process so much fun. Your covers, ideas, graphics, art. Every. Fucking. Thing. Is beyond beautiful. I'm so happy to have 'met' you and that I get to call you my friend. So, so much love for you, you're stuck with me forever and a day.

Kristen - for Alpha-ing the shit out of this and finding all my missing words. For your songs, your snaps, your video-calls, shopping hauls and dirty fucking *everything*. I love you diehard.

Dily - for never failing to make me laugh, smile, cry, or do the Muttley snigger! I love you and your spoons so much, thank you for always making me so happy.

Kendal - I love you. Words will never be enough.

🖤

ALSO BY K.L. TAYLOR-LANE

SWALLOWS AND PSYCHOS

KYLA-ROSE SWALLOW

A Dark Mafia Why Choose Romance

PURGATORY

PENANCE

PERSECUTION

CHARLIE SWALLOW

A Dark Mafia MMF Romance

RUIN

THE BLACKWELL BROTHERS

HUNTER BLACKWELL

A Dark Gothic Horror-esque Stepsibling MF Romance

HERON MILL

HERON MILL - TENEBRIS

THORNE BLACKWELL

A Dark Gothic Mafia MF Romance

ROOK POINT

THE ASHES BOYS

A Dark Bully Gang Why Choose Romance

TORMENT ME

BURY ME

FIND K.L. TAYLOR-LANE

BOOKBUB - @KLTaylorLane

AMAZON - K. L. TAYLOR-LANE

INSTAGRAM - @kltaylorlane_author

TIKTOK - @kltaylorlane.author

PINTEREST - @KLTaylorLane

FACEBOOK - K. L. Taylor-Lane Author

GOODREADS - kltaylor-lane

READER GROUP - KL's Southbrook Psychos

Made in the USA
Middletown, DE
26 February 2024